W9-BRQ-144

ONE AGAINST SIX

Fargo cursed as he drew the Colt. He wanted answers, not a gunfight. But they were leaving him no choice. The one called Jake was atop the girl, pushing her legs apart with one knee as she struggled. She had little chance with the other one holding her arms. Fargo raised the Colt and took aim. The man fighting with the girl was moving too much to risk a shot, and Fargo chose the ones standing by looking on. He fired three times, and three of the men suddenly jerked where they stood, as if they'd been seized with spasms. Two fell against each other as they went down; the third spun and collapsed in a heap where he stood. The mustached one atop the girl swung from her and yanked his gun out as he cursed.

Fargo saw the girl roll. But the three remaining attackers were firing, pouring lead into the trees. Fargo ducked as bullets hurtled all around him. . . .

SIGNET

THRILLING ADVENTURES FROM THE TRAILSMAN

☐ **THE TRAILSMAN #157: GHOST RANCH MASSACRE by Jon Sharpe.** Skye Fargo figured he was heading into danger when he answered a call for help from his old pal Hank Griffin. Hank wasn't the kind to scare easy—but even so, the horror that Fargo ran into in the terror-haunted mountains of Arizona was hard to believe and even harder to battle. (181611—$3.99)

☐ **THE TRAILSMAN #158: TEXAS TERROR by Jon Sharpe.** Skye Fargo was hunting the two most vicious killers in the Lone Star state, and he'd have to draw fast and shoot faster to outgun those mad-dog murderers. But the Trailsman was caught with his gun belt off and his guard down in the dusty town of Ripclaw. (182154—$3.99)

☐ **THE TRAILSMAN #159: NORTH COUNTRY GUNS by Jon Sharpe.** When a call for help from an old friend draws Skye Fargo north to Canadian Saskatchewan, he finds himself facing a tribe of killer Crees, a pack of poachers who piled up corpses as high as pelts, and a mysterious mastermind carving out an empire of evil victim by victim. (182162—$3.99)

☐ **THE TRAILSMAN #160: THE TORNADO TRAIL by Jon Sharpe.** When Skye Fargo pledges to lead a beautiful widow's herd of cattle and her rag-tag crew along a twisting Oklahoma trail, he does not depend on the notorious drunk Quince Porterfield to enlist him in the hunt for a kidnapped Choctaw girl. Now all Fargo can hope for is that he doesn't leave them all twisting in the wind at the first wrong turn. (182170—$3.99)

*Prices slightly higher in Canada

Buy them at your local bookstore or use this convenient coupon for ordering.

PENGUIN USA
P.O. Box 999 — Dept. #17109
Bergenfield, New Jersey 07621

Please send me the books I have checked above.
I am enclosing $_____ (please add $2.00 to cover postage and handling). Send check or money order (no cash or C.O.D.'s) or charge by Mastercard or VISA (with a $15.00 minimum). Prices and numbers are subject to change without notice.

Card #_____ Exp. Date _____
Signature_____
Name_____
Address_____
City _____ State _____ Zip Code _____

For faster service when ordering by credit card call **1-800-253-6476**

Allow a minimum of 4-6 weeks for delivery. This offer is subject to change without notice.

THE
TRAILSMAN
#196

KANSAS
CARNAGE

by
Jon Sharpe

A SIGNET BOOK

SIGNET
Published by the Penguin Group
Penguin Putnam Inc., 375 Hudson Street,
New York, New York 10014, U.S.A.
Penguin Books Ltd, 27 Wrights Lane,
London W8 5TZ, England
Penguin Books Australia Ltd,
Ringwood, Victoria, Australia
Penguin Books Canada Ltd, 10 Alcorn Avenue,
Toronto, Ontario, Canada M4V 3B2
Penguin Books (N.Z.) Ltd, 182–190 Wairau Road,
Auckland 10, New Zealand

Penguin Books Ltd, Registered Offices:
Harmondsworth, Middlesex, England

First published by Signet,
an imprint of Dutton Signet,
a member of Penguin Putnam Inc.

First Printing, April, 1998
10 9 8 7 6 5 4 3 2 1

Copyright © Jon Sharpe, 1998
All rights reserved

Ⓢ REGISTERED TRADEMARK—MARCA REGISTRADA

Printed in the United States of America

Without limiting the rights under copyright reserved above, no part of this
publication may be reproduced, stored in or introduced into a retrieval system, or
transmitted, in any form, or by any means (electronic, mechanical, photocopying,
recording, or otherwise), without the prior written permission of both the copyright
owner and the above publisher of this book.

BOOKS ARE AVAILABLE AT QUANTITY DISCOUNTS WHEN USED TO PROMOTE PRODUCTS OR
SERVICES. FOR INFORMATION PLEASE WRITE TO PREMIUM MARKETING DIVISION, PENGUIN
PUTNAM INC., 375 HUDSON STREET, NY, NEW YORK 10014.

If you purchased this book without a cover you should be aware that this book is
stolen property. It was reported as "unsold and destroyed" to the publisher and
neither the author nor the publisher has received any payment for this "stripped
book."

The Trailsman

Beginnings ... they bend the tree and they mark the man. Skye Fargo was born when he was eighteen. Terror was his midwife, vengeance his first cry. Killing spawned Skye Fargo, ruthless, cold-blooded murder. Out of the acrid smoke of gunpowder still hanging in the air, he rose, cried out a promise never forgotten.

The Trailsman they began to call him all across the West: searcher, scout, hunter, the man who could see where others only looked, his skills for hire but not his soul, the man who lived each day to the fullest, yet trailed each tomorrow. Skye Fargo, the Trailsman, and the seeker who could take the wildness of a land and the wanting of a woman and make them his own.

*1860, near the Smoky Hills
of the Kansas Territory, where old
ambitions are given new meaning by
a deadly game of deceit and dishonor
that threatens to set the great
prairies on fire. . . .*

1

It was a lesson he had learned long ago. He hadn't forgotten it, he just had not paid enough attention to it. But the morning made him remember. In a single, heart-wrenching moment, it made him remember.

The morning sounds were always wonderful harbingers, the voices of the songbirds, the black-capped chickadee, the horned lark and the redwing, the busy, scurrying sounds of the fox squirrels, prairie dogs, and gophers, all offering comfort. The morning smells were next, the ever-new scent of the dew-wet grass, the special, rich odor of the soil waking to the sun, the full, slightly sweet aroma of the black walnut seeds. These odors, like the sounds, could make the morning a warm and welcoming embrace.

But the morning sounds and smells were not enough. There was a third element. It took the harshness of seeing to make the morning complete, the unforgiving reality of everything given shape and form, sounds and smells made real. It had happened before and now it happened again. He had wakened, washed in the brook, and was almost finished dressing when the column of smoke rose from the horizon, just over the distant hills. A sudden, silent intrusion that spiraled upward, piercing the sweetness of the morning as a dagger pierces a cloak. Skye Fargo's lake blue eyes narrowed as he saw the column of smoke rise into the air. To the Trailsman, a column of smoke was not simply a column of smoke. Like every other sign, print, mark, and trail, it spoke, in its own way, with its own voice. Campfire smoke was erratic and fitful and came apart in the air. Smoke from a brushfire was stringy and spread quickly. Smoke from a burning wagon was white to gray-white. Smoke from a burning house was thick and dark gray to black.

Fargo felt the curse catch in his throat as he watched the column of smoke grow thicker and blacker. He was buckling on his gunbelt as he raced across the ground to where the Ovaro grazed in a patch of downy brome-grass. Flinging the saddle over the pure white back of the horse, he yanked the cinch tight and vaulted onto the horse. In moments, the Ovaro was galloping toward the hills, its jet black fore-and-hindquarters glistening in the morning sun. He sent the horse in a direct line toward the column of smoke and when he began to descend over the last low hill, he turned right into a stand of bur oak. The land flattened out as he neared the bottom of the hill; it then became more open, but Fargo stayed inside the trees.

He heard the high-pitched shouts and whoops before the house came into sight, burning fiercely, the thick black column of smoke still rising from it. He was actually glad to see the near-naked horsemen on their short-legged Indian ponies racing back and forth. It meant their grim business was still unfinished and he saw the reason why as they poured arrows into a small, flat-roofed, solid stone structure a dozen yards from the burning house. The family, at least all those left alive, had taken refuge in their cold-storage house built to keep grain and other perishables away from the rodent population. Fargo drew the pinto to a halt, reached back, and pulled the big Henry from its saddlecase. He took a quick count as he brought the rifle to his shoulder. There were ten or twelve racing horsemen. Staying in the trees, he fired two shots and saw two of the attackers fly from their ponies. Another figure crossed in front of his gunsight and he fired again. The Indian toppled sideways from his pony and Fargo saw the others begin to peel away in two directions.

They wheeled and half circled in surprise and alarm. Fargo held his fire. The Indian didn't like surprises. He liked being trapped even less. But most of all, he disliked the unknown enemy, who they were, how many, if there were more on the way. They peered into the trees as they backed and circled but they still hesitated. Fargo moved the pinto sideways some dozen feet, fired again, moved sideways again, and fired. One of the attackers pitched to the ground. It was enough for the others. Unsure how many attackers were in the trees, they decided on retreat. One, a young buck, wheeled his pony in a tight circle as he brought his arm down in a short, chopping motion. The others followed him as he raced away.

Fargo peered at the fleeing riders and focused on the armband of one. "Pawnee," he muttered as he saw the distinctive decorative patterns that the Pawnee favored. He stayed in the trees, listened until he was satisfied that they were gone, and slowly nosed the Ovaro out of the oaks. He rode to the stone storehouse and dismounted before the door opened. A man stepped out, his face tight with fear and strain, an old Hawkens plains rifle in his hands as he stared at Fargo.

"Just you, mister?" he said.

"Just me," Fargo said.

"Jesus, from the way they were dropping I thought there were at least half a dozen of you," the man said.

"That's what they decided." Fargo smiled and the

door opened wider to reveal a woman and two small boys. Fargo's glance went over the four of them. "Anybody else?" he asked.

"No, just us. We were lucky. We saw them coming and got in here in time," the man said. "But they'd have gotten to us sooner or later if you hadn't come by. We'll be owing you forever, mister. I'm Jed Harrison and this is my wife, Martha, my boys, Ted and Terence."

"Fargo, Skye Fargo," the Trailsman said.

"I'm worried about the Beeneys," Martha Harrison said as she stepped from the stone storage house. "They live a mile north. Those stinking savages came at us from the north."

"I'll go see," Fargo said. "Meanwhile, you stay here in your storage house. It's the best place for you until I find out more."

"You think they'll be coming back?" Jed Harrison asked.

"No, but you can't ever be sure about Indians. You stay holed up here. I'll be back," Fargo said and pulled himself onto the horse. He waited till the Harrisons retreated back into the storage house and closed the door before he rode away. His path followed the Pawnee tracks north until they turned and rode west. They hadn't slowed, their prints still digging deep into the ground, he saw, and he felt relief for that much. But the relief didn't last. It ended as he crested a low rise and came onto the Beeney house. What was left of the Beeney house, he corrected himself, a blackened pile of still-smoldering logs. Outside lay the bodies of a man, a woman, and three children. He halted, swung to the ground, and went from one still form to the other, hoping to find life still clinging to someone. But he found only brutal death. Terrible things had been done to the woman before she was killed. The man, too. And the oldest of the children, a young girl. They were the kind of things that marked fury and rage.

When he walked back to his horse, his frown dug deeply into his brow. He knew the Pawnee. Like most of the warrior Plains tribes, they were savage fighters and clever, resourceful attackers. They could be fierce and cruel, giving no quarter and asking none. This was their way, the warrior's way. But what he saw here had a different feel to it, a stamp of viciousness that was beyond the Pawnee way. More than fighting back, it bore the stamp of retaliation and the frown stayed with him as he climbed onto the Ovaro and rode back across the hills.

He reached the Harrisons to find the fire had burned itself down to smoldering ashes. The family came out of the storage house at once, the woman peering hard at him. "Oh my God," she murmured, reading the set of his face. "Oh my God. All of them?"

Fargo nodded. "Get together whatever you've left. You can't stay here," he said.

"Maybe they won't hit us again. Maybe this was just a raid. We can rebuild," Jed Harrison said.

Fargo tried to keep the impatience from his voice and knew he didn't succeed. "This was no ordinary raid. Get your things. We've no time to waste talking," he said and watched as the family began to salvage what little they could, a trunk that had resisted burning, a strong box no doubt filled with family papers, some clothes that had hung on a clothesline off by itself. Jed Harrison brought out a standard utility one-horse farm wagon that had been in a wooden shed back of the trees. They loaded their few remaining possessions into it, then the youngsters climbed in as Harrison took the reins. Fargo rode ahead a few hundred yards, surveyed the terrain, saw nothing to bother him, and fell back to ride alongside the wagon. The sight of the Beeney home stayed with him. "How many more families in these parts?" he asked.

"Just Ed and Sarah Culligan. They're south of here," Harrison said.

"We're going south. We'll stop there," Fargo said.

"I've been afraid this was coming," Martha Harrison put in.

"Why?" Fargo frowned.

"We've seen so many more of them lately, more than we ever have. They kept their distance but they kept coming by, gave me the shivers every time," the woman said. "Where are you taking us?"

"There's a fort south of here," Fargo said.

"Army post. Fort Travis. But that's a few days' ride," Jed Harrison said. "There's no hiding place out here, Fargo."

"I'm hoping to catch sight of a platoon on patrol. They can escort you to the fort," Fargo said.

"Haven't seen any of those around in some while," the man said.

"What made you settle out this far? You're way past what the army calls safe land," Fargo said. "Not that their safe land is so safe."

"Good land for the taking," Harrison said. "We figured the army patrols that came this far would keep things peaceable. Seems they did until lately."

Fargo turned the man's answer over in his mind. Good land for the taking, he echoed silently, a dream of naive, trusting souls and of stubborn, thickheaded fools. It didn't much matter which they were. Maybe a little of both. But it was the other things he had said that bothered Fargo. Things had been peaceable and now suddenly they were not. The Great Plains were always a tinderbox, always a place where sudden beauty and sudden death existed side by side. But what he had seen this morning with his own eyes, and had heard from Jed Harrison's lips, hinted at something more, events that cast shadows. But shadows of what? He had no idea. He knew only one thing. He didn't like it. He knew how fast a prairie fire could erupt and consume everything in its path. The fires of hate and rage could spread just as fast.

He pushed these thoughts away and his eyes scanned the ground as he rode. There were unshod pony prints all over, too many for just hunting parties. They were approaching a dip in the land, box elder, and black oak thick across the terrain when the rifle shots erupted. "Oh, no, oh God," Martha Harrison screamed at once. "Down there, that's the Culligan place."

"Get under your wagon and stay there," Fargo barked as he reached back, pulling the big Henry from its case. He spurred the Ovaro forward and swerved the horse through the black oak as more rifle shots sounded. He rode hard down the incline until the land flattened and he saw the cleared area, the house and barn in the center. A half-dozen loincloth-garbed riders were pouring arrows into the house. Rifle fire came from two of the windows, sporadic and wide of the racing horsemen. These weren't the ones that had attacked the Harrisons, Fargo saw at once. They were all young bucks and they lacked the experience and controlled purpose of the others, their assault was more exuberant than effective. Fargo drew a bead on one as he halted the pinto, fired, and the Indian flew sideways from his pony. The others turned at once. It took but a split second for them to see the figure on the ground and they streaked away in all directions. Fargo sent a shot after them as they fled into the trees behind the house. After listening for a moment, he was satisfied they were racing away.

He moved the pinto into the open and the door of the house opened. A man, a teenage boy, and a woman came from the house, both the man and the boy holding old army carbines. "You alone, mister," the man called out.

"Your neighbors, Jed and Martha Harrison, are back a ways," Fargo said. "You're Culligan."

"That's right. This is Jeff Carter. He came to work for me last week," Ed Culligan said.

"I don't think I'll be staying," the boy said, his face chalk white.

"Nobody's staying," Fargo said. "Get together what you want to take. The Harrisons were wiped out. The Beeneys killed."

"Dear God," Sarah Culligan whispered.

"Same ones that just hit us?" Culligan asked.

"No, others. A lot worse," Fargo said.

"Why all of a sudden? They haven't bothered us until now," the man blurted out in exasperation.

"I always heard Indians don't need a lot of fancy reasons," the youth muttered.

He wasn't entirely wrong, Fargo thought to himself. Yet there were reasons here. He felt it inside him as he thought back to the scene at the Beeneys'. No sudden, random explosion, not this. "I'll fetch the Harrisons. Get yourselves ready to go," he said as he turned the Ovaro and rode back up the incline. The Harrisons were under their wagon when he reached them and he gave an approving nod as they emerged. They followed him back to the Culligans, where he found a freight wagon outfitted with stake sides. Sarah Culligan sat inside it amid a welter of boxes and trunks. Ed Culligan held the reins of a two-horse brace and the boy, Jeff, waited astride an old roan with a graying mask.

They exchanged greetings with the Harrisons, a grim and unhappy meeting, and fell in beside each other as Fargo rode ahead. Once again, he scanned the terrain and saw too many unshod hoofprints. An object on the ground caught his eye and he halted, dismounted, and picked up a torn piece of moccasin. The frown came to his face as he examined it. It wasn't Pawnee, he saw, staring at it for a long moment. The Pawnee made their moccasins with a double seam along the side of the sole. His lips pulled back in distaste, he pushed the piece of deerskin into the pocket of his jacket and returned to the saddle.

He wouldn't go rushing to conclusions, he told himself. Besides, he hadn't enough to do that. But he was growing more and more apprehensive, he admitted as he put the pinto into a trot. The land thinned out and became clusters of hackberry as the sun moved into late afternoon. He paused occasionally at a high place to let the wagons see him before riding on again. The day was beginning to draw to a close when he saw the movement of branches along a stand of hackberry. They moved in a straight, steady line and he sent the Ovaro forward. The blue-clad uniforms appeared and began to turn to go back the way they had come. Fargo shouted as he spurred the horse on and he frowned as he saw but six troopers, an officer at the head of the group.

The officer saw him and drew to a halt as Fargo rode up. "You're riding hard, mister," the officer said, a lieutenant's bar on his shoulder. Fargo took in a young, earnest face, blond hair reaching down beneath his cap, and a small, blond mustache that was unable to add maturity to his unlined face.

"Trouble," Fargo said. "Two families are following me. A third didn't live to run."

"Indian attacks?" the lieutenant said, his face tightening.

Fargo nodded. "Been looking to find a patrol. Where's the rest of your platoon?"

"There is none. This is it. I'm Lieutenant Roswall."

"A six-man platoon?" Fargo asked incredulously.

"That's right," the lieutenant said.

"That's crazy," Fargo blurted out. "Who the hell ordered that?"

"General Cogwell at Fort Travis," Lieutenant Roswall said, keeping his voice flat.

"A six-man platoon's like the tits on a bull, not good for anything," Fargo said.

"We've orders only to reconnoiter. We're supposed to avoid engaging the Indians," the lieutenant said.

"What if they engage you?" Fargo snapped.

"We run," Lieutenant Roswall said grimly.

"If you can," Fargo said. "This is the damned stupidest thing I ever heard."

"Generals decide field policy, not lieutenants," Roswall said. "I was about to turn back. I've come out further than I'm supposed to go."

Fargo was still shaking his head in wonder as the two wagons rolled into view. "I was looking for an escort to get these people to the fort," he said.

"We'll take them," the officer said.

Fargo snorted. "Hell of a piss-poor escort," he said. "Nothing personal."

The lieutenant shrugged. "Sorry. Can't do any better," he said and Fargo heard the apology in his voice.

"No, you can't. Guess I'll ride along with you. I'll be one more gun in case they decide to jump us," Fargo said.

"Let's hope they don't," Lieutenant Roswall said. "There haven't been any raids near the fort."

"Guess the trouble's back north across the plains," Fargo said and brought the Ovaro alongside the lieutenant as the rest of the troopers flanked the two wagons. The little procession moved south, staying near the hackberry, and Fargo still felt the anger pushing at him.

"Why the reconnaissance patrols?" he asked the lieutenant.

"Guess General Cogwell wants to know what's going on anywhere near the fort," Roswall said.

"He could send out scouts to do that," Fargo said. "If he sends out a platoon it ought to be able to take care of itself, at least."

"The general's keeping most of the troops in and around the fort," Roswall said.

"Why? He expecting trouble?" Fargo queried.

"I asked that," the lieutenant answered. "He said no. He just wanted a strong deterrent force at the fort just in case." Fargo snorted and decided to drop the matter as the day came to an end. They made camp alongside the hackberry. Fargo took a while before he slept, the events of the day still clinging, not so much for themselves but for what they might mean. But finally he slept and in the morning they resumed the journey after sharing army breakfast rations. They made better time than he expected and it was still light as they neared Fort Travis.

Settlers' houses began to appear, spread out with plenty of farmland between them. The road wound its way through the new homes that grew more plentiful as they neared the fort. Fargo saw the fort itself come into sight, took in a good-enough stockade fence but no corner blockhouses. Sturdy enough, yet no major fort such as Pitt or Laramie, he saw the stables and barracks were contained inside the stockade walls. He also saw a line of army tents outside the stockade. The general was definitely taking precautions, unusual ones for someone who didn't expect trouble. As troopers escorted the Harrisons and Culligans inside the fort, Lieutenant Roswall paused beside Fargo. "Come along while I report to the general," he said.

"Fine," Fargo said and followed the young officer into the separate building that was the general's quarters. He waited as the lieutenant made his report. When he was called, Fargo stepped into the inner office. "This is the man who saved two of the families," Roswall said.

"Skye Fargo," the Trailsman said. His glance took in a tall man in a sharply pressed uniform, graying hair atop a face that was coldly handsome, a stiff, unbending quality to it. General Cogwell had a well-built frame, a trim body, and blue eyes that were as cold as they were piercing. His thin lips had difficulty offering a smile that was not sardonic.

"Skye Fargo, I know that name," General Cogwell said, peering at Fargo as he let his lips purse. "I make a point of remembering names. Give me a few moments."

"You make a point of small platoons," Fargo said.

General Cogwell returned a tolerant smile. "You disapprove?" he said.

"Can't understand why," Fargo said. "You've plenty of troops here at the fort."

"Precautions. I believe in precautions."

"Seems to me like you're expecting trouble."

"I certainly hope not. But I'm not charged with keeping the territory peaceful, just protecting Fort Travis," the general said. "General Miles Davis is in charge of keeping peace." He stopped and snapped his fingers loudly. "That's it, Fargo. You're an old friend of Miles Davis. You've worked for him, scouted for him."

"That's right," Fargo said. "You keep track of things."

"I make it my business to. You see General Davis lately, Fargo?" Cogwell asked.

"No, not in a while," Fargo answered.

"It's his job to keep peace in the territory, you know. I just hope he's doing the job he's supposed to be doing," Cogwell said.

"I know Miles Davis. I'm sure he is," Fargo said.

General Cogwell's smile was laced with condescension. "The two families you brought might not agree with you," he said.

"Perhaps not," Fargo had to concede. "Makes me real curious as to what's going on. Maybe I'll pay General Davis a visit."

Cogwell's voice grew cold. "I consider that entirely unnecessary, actually quite useless," he said and Fargo's irritation rose at the man's tone.

"I consider six-man platoons pretty damn useless," Fargo said and saw the general's face stiffen.

"I decide what's appropriate around here," Cogwell said.

"And I decide who I'll visit," Fargo returned.

"You may show Mr. Fargo out, Lieutenant," Cogwell said.

"It's been a real pleasure," Fargo said as he walked from the office with the lieutenant at his side. Outside, Roswall offered an apologetic shrug.

"The general can be difficult to deal with," the young officer said.

"Me, too." Fargo smiled, pulled himself onto the Ovaro, and swept the inside of the fort with a long glance. "What'll he do with the two families?" Fargo asked.

"Put them up, maybe with some of the other families for now," Roswall said.

"Thanks for getting them here," Fargo said.

"Glad I could help," the lieutenant said.

"If General Davis is in charge of keeping peace in the territory he's got to be set up somewhere on the plains. You know where, Lieutenant?" Fargo asked.

"He's set up a field camp along the Smoky Hill River," Roswall said. "Smack in the middle of Pawnee country."

"That'd be Miles Davis." Fargo chuckled. "Let the enemy see you're not afraid. Much obliged, Lieutenant. Good luck."

"Same to you, Fargo," Roswall said. Fargo moved the pinto through the fort at a walk and out through the houses that stretched outside the fort. He paused to glance at the line of army pup tents that ran outside the stockade walls. It was a strange, almost incongruous scene, Fargo decided. General Cogwell was plainly very concerned about the safety of the fort and the community that stretched out beyond it. He had a heavy complement of troops inside the fort and extra soldiers set up outside. Why was he so big on precautions yet willing to sent out six-man platoons that weren't much use for anything except targets?

It made no sense and was as unexplainable as the eruption of hate and rage he had seen yesterday morning. Fargo was still seeking some reason when the day descended and he found a spot to bed down in a thicket of black oak. But he'd decided one thing. He would definitely pay Miles Davis a visit. It had been a long time since he'd seen the general and now he had one more reason. It wasn't often he was close enough for a visit. But as he settled down on his bedroll, Fargo knew one more thing. He'd not be riding with casual ease.

22

Something was brewing on the Kansas prairie. He felt its long, grim shadow as he finally slept.

2

The day came in sunny and after breakfasting on a stand of wild plums, Fargo rode northeast. He continued to see numerous trails of pony prints but nothing more as the great Kansas plains stretched out before him. Riding leisurely, he crossed the Arkansas where it joined Bear Creek and turned north, riding until the sun crossed the noon sky and he saw a gentle rise thick with hackberry and some red oak mixed in. He took the rise and rode into the trees to get out of the burning sun. At a stream, he halted and let the Ovaro drink before moving on. Staying in the trees, he felt the rise grow steeper and he rode at the edge of the trees and found himself looking down at the land below.

The movement of leaves caught his eye and he watched as the horsemen appeared, their blue uniforms almost blending in with the dark green of the hackberry leaves. Six troopers, another of Cogwell's six-man platoons. Fargo found himself frowning down at the troop. These were a hell of a lot farther out than Roswall's squad had been. The lieutenant had said they were under orders to patrol only a limited parameter from the fort. Fargo's frown stayed as he kept pace with the platoon below and he felt the frown digging deeper into his forehead. Something about the six troopers bothered him. It took him a few minutes of observing to define it but it finally defined itself. They didn't ride like troopers. Staying slightly behind them, he edged the Ovaro closer to the tree line.

They didn't sit their horses like U.S. cavalrymen. They slouched in the saddle. Troopers rode with their backs straight, even when they were exhausted. It was drilled into them until it was part of them. These six rode in a ragged line, he noted. U.S. cavalrymen didn't ride in a ragged line. His eyes narrowed and grew ice blue. They wore troopers' uniforms, army boots. They could pass as troopers to the average observer but they weren't U.S. cavalry. What were they? The question pushed at him and he dropped back before sending the Ovaro down the slope. Keeping his eyes on the six horsemen, he swung in behind, following them as they moved deeper into the woods.

They stayed in the trees until the forest began to thin out. Staying behind, yet close enough to see, Fargo saw an open field as he peered past the six men. The riders slowed as they neared the field. Fargo slowed with them and moved to the right to get a clearer view of the field. Four squaws were in the center of the field, which was an almost unbroken carpet of white-capped meadow mushrooms. They were busy gathering mushrooms and putting them into cloth sacks.

Another glance at the four squaws showed that three were older women with square, bulky figures, but the fourth was young and trim with jet black hair flowing down her back. She wore the usual two-piece elkskin dress, but with a rawhide belt around the waist that outlined high breasts and narrow hips. Fargo's eyes went to the six horsemen. One raised his hand in a signal which sent all six horses racing out of the trees and onto the field. The Pawnee squaws whirled in surprise and started to run, two of the older women falling and

25

spilling their mushrooms as they did. But the six horsemen were paying no attention to them. They converged on the young woman. Two of them reached her first, closed in on her, and rode her down. The one reached over, grabbed her by the long, jet hair, causing her to scream out in pain. He yanked back and she half fell, but the other one leaned over, scooped her up, and pulled her onto his horse.

Fargo had the Colt out but held back firing. There was no way he could get a shot at the two riders without possibly hitting the girl. He swore silently. Two of the fake troopers rode alongside the one holding the young woman and the other three rode behind. All six made a circle around the three older squaws, who looked on in surprise and fear. But they made no move toward the three women except to circle them, almost as if they were taunting them with their prize. Then, to Fargo's surprise, they turned and raced off with the Indian girl, leaving the three older squaws untouched.

Fargo waited until they disappeared into the cluster of hackberry on the other side of the mushroom field. Holstering the Colt, he waited until they were well into the trees before he sent the Ovaro out across the field. The three older women were running away as he raced past them and into the trees on the other side. Once inside the hackberry, he slowed down to listen to the sound of the horsemen as they moved through the woods. He followed his ears and when he caught sight of the blue-clad riders bunched together, he slowed and hung back. The questions tumbled through his mind as he followed the horsemen.

Why were they masquerading as troopers? That was the first question. Why did they seize the Indian girl? They hadn't just come upon her. They had sought her out; the attack had been planned. But why just her?

Why leave the other three squaws untouched to watch and then run? No happenstance. No coincidence. Who the hell were they? He'd find out, he promised himself as he trailed the six fake troopers. They rode another fifteen minutes until they reached a small glen of soft dropseed grass with a border of doveweeds which opened up in the trees. The men halted, swung from their horses, and flung the Indian girl to the ground. Fargo had a chance to look at her properly for the first time. She had a face with none of the usual heavy Pawnee features, no wide nose, no broad face. Instead, she had a straight, thin nose, high cheekbones, finely etched lips, and an acorn brown skin that glowed. She was a very handsome young woman. More than handsome, he corrected himself; there was something close to a regalness in her face.

Her eyes flashed only contempt at the six men who gathered around her in a half circle. "We take care of her now?" one asked.

A tall man with an unkempt mustache licked his lips. "Seems to me we ought to enjoy ourselves first," he said.

"Now you're talking, Jake," another said. The mustached one reached down, grabbed a handful of the girl's jet black hair, and pulled her to her feet. Fargo saw the pain go through her face but she refused to cry out.

"Pigs," she threw at them.

The man voiced Fargo's surprise. "Well, look here, she can talk English," he said. One of the others suddenly seized her from behind and the mustached one stepped toward her, dodged a kick she aimed at him, and pulled the rawhide belt from her waist. With a quick motion, he flung the elkskin dress up and over her head, pulled it free of her arms and flung it aside. Fargo glimpsed shapely, lithe legs, a flash of upturned breasts, and then

27

the man was on her, pushing her to the ground and falling over her. "Hold her damn arms," he yelled and one of the others grabbed the girl's wrists, pulled her arms upward.

"Give it to her, Jake," another called. "Hurry up. I'm next."

Fargo cursed as he drew the Colt. He wanted answers, not a gunfight. But they were leaving him no choice. The one called Jake was atop the girl, pushing her legs apart with one knee as she struggled. But she had little chance with the other one holding her arms. Fargo raised the Colt and took aim. The man fighting with the girl was moving too much to risk a shot, so Fargo chose the ones standing by. He fired three shots and three of the men suddenly jerked where they stood, as if they'd been seized with spasms. Two fell against each other as they went down, the third jerked and spun and collapsed in a heap where ne stood. The mustached one atop the girl swung from her and yanked his gun out as he cursed.

Fargo saw the girl roll and push to her knees. He glimpsed a tight little rear as she scrambled to reach the dress. But the three remaining attackers were firing, pouring lead into the trees where his shots had come from and Fargo ducked as bullets hurtled all around him. He found a moment to fire again and one of the three groaned as he pitched forward, the gun falling from his hand. The mustached one had dived to his left and was pulling himself into the saddle from the other side of the horse. The sixth one was also climbing onto his horse, and flattening themselves in the saddle, both men raced for the trees only a few yards away.

They were at the hackberry in seconds as Fargo fired and heard the cry of pain and the curse. But the two horses kept going, the foliage instantly closing around them in a leafy curtain. Fargo turned to the young squaw and saw that she had pulled the elkskin dress on. Her black eyes held him as they searched his face. She gazed at him with a mixture of gratefulness and uncertainty. The Pawnee spoke mostly Caddoan, a language Fargo didn't know nearly as well as he did the Siouan or Shoshone. But she had spoken one word of English. Perhaps she knew more. "Can you speak the white man's tongue?" he asked. Her shoulders lifted in a half shrug and she made the sign language gesture for small. "A little," he said and she nodded. "I must go after them. You stay here," he said. She did not answer and continued to search his face. "Do not run away. I will come back. I will take you home," he said. She didn't answer. "Do you understand?" he asked, using some sign language.

"Yes," she finally said, nodding. The answer seemed a decision on her part with almost a tolerant concession in it. He turned and pulled himself onto the Ovaro.

"Stay," he repeated as he sent the horse into the trees. Inside the forest he peered at the leaves of the low branches as well as the ground and quickly spotted the drops of blood. He followed the trail and noticed that they had slowed. The one he'd winged was losing a lot of blood, the trail growing increasingly easy to follow. He soon heard the sounds of the horses moving almost at a walk and he slowed as he moved after them. The two figures came into view minutes later and he was drawing closer when one of the two pitched forward in the saddle and toppled from his horse.

He lay unmoving on the ground and Fargo saw the mustached man halt, wait, and stare down at the prone figure. Dismounting, the man bent down to the figure, extracted a roll of bills from his pocket, and shoved them into his shirt. Then he pulled himself back onto his horse. He started to go on when Fargo drew his Colt and sent the pinto charging forward. The man half turned in the saddle, surprise flooding his face. He started to reach for his gun. "I wouldn't do that," Fargo said, pulling to a halt. The man's hand froze and dropped to his side as he saw the barrel of the Colt staring him in the face. "Now take the gun out, two fingers only, and throw it on the ground," Fargo ordered. The man obeyed, his eye on the Colt as he did. "Get down," Fargo snapped, swinging from the Ovaro as the man dismounted. "Talk, mister. You're not cavalry. Why the disguise? Who the hell are you?" Fargo asked.

"How do you know we're not cavalry?" The man glowered.

"Same way I know a decoy from a mallard," Fargo said. "Talk." The man's mouth thinned into a tight line as he refused to answer. "The right answer is the only thing that will keep you alive," Fargo said. The man maintained his truculent silence. "I figure I've got maybe another thirty seconds of patience left," Fargo said.

"I talk and you kill me anyway," the man said.

"You talk and you walk," Fargo said.

"Sure. You think I'm gonna believe that?" the man said.

Fargo grunted. The man was a small-time criminal, the kind that lived his life with distrust. He wasn't about to change now. He could face death easier than he could bring himself to trust anyone. The incongruity of it was a strange twist of human nature. But there was something else about the type Fargo had discovered long ago. Death was a condition, almost an abstract reality, beyond really grasping. But pain was something else. Pain was no abstraction. Pain was immediate. Only the very strong could cope with pain, the strong outside and inside. Fargo's eyes bored into the mustached face.

There was no strength in it. Distrust, cynicism, fatalism, greed, stupidity, but no strength. "Once more. Talk and you can walk," Fargo said.

"Tell me another," the man flung back.

Fargo let the Colt drop down an inch. When he fired, the man screamed as he fell, clutching at his left kneecap with both hands. "Oh Jesus . . . oh Christ . . . owooooo," he cried out as he rolled on the ground. "My goddamn kneecap. Oh Jesus, it hurts. Goddamn, it hurts."

"That's only for starters," Fargo said. "Every part of you is going to hurt so much you'll wish you were dead."

"Bastard. Son of a bitch," the man bit out between gasps of pain as he continued to clutch at his knee.

"Talk," Fargo said.

"Go to hell," the man flung back in fury and pain. Fargo raised the Colt and fired. The shot slammed into the man's shoulder and knocked him onto his back. "Owoooo, oh Christ . . . oh God," he screamed, one hand clutching his shoulder, his shattered kneecap pulled up with his other hand.

"I think we'll do the other kneecap next," Fargo said and shifted the Colt.

"No, oh Christ no more," the man cried out as he writhed on the ground. "No, I can't take any more."

"Talk," Fargo said. "Why'd you take the girl?"

"It was a job. We got paid for it," the man said between groans.

"To take the girl only?" Fargo asked and the man nodded. "Who paid you?"

"He didn't give his name."

"What'd he look like?"

"Short, heavy-set, wore a suit."

"You didn't just happen on her."

"He told us where we'd find her, said they always picked mushrooms there. Jesus, I need a doc," the man said.

"Where'd he hire you?" Fargo questioned.

"West, other side of Mount Sunflower."

"Why the uniforms?"

"He wanted us to wear them, gave them to us."

"Why?"

"Don't know. We didn't ask."

"Why just the girl?" Fargo pressed.

"Don't know. Those were his orders," the man said and groaned again in pain. "A doc, get me a goddamn doc."

Fargo stared at him for another moment and decided he wasn't lying and didn't know anything more. "Find one yourself," he said and pulled himself onto the Ovaro.

"No, you can't leave me here. I can't ride, goddamn you," the man shouted.

"A man can do amazing things when he has to," Fargo said as he turned the horse and started to ride away. He heard the curses mingled with the groans behind him, then a sudden, sharp scream of rage and pain, a special fury in it. He turned and saw that the man had flung himself forward despite the pain wracking his body, his hand closing over the gun on the ground.

"Goddamn bastard," he screamed as he fired. Fargo ducked a bullet that passed over him. He yanked his Colt out as another shot was wide but closer. "I'll kill you, you son of a bitch," the man swore as he fired again. The shot passed to the left and Fargo's Colt barked twice. The figure on the ground jerked violently, shuddered, and lay still.

Fargo moved a few paces toward him. "Damn fool," he muttered. "I gave you more of a chance than you'd have given her." He holstered as he rode away, hurrying the horse through the hackberry as he wondered if the girl would be there. When he reached the clearing and saw only mushrooms, he shrugged, not surprised. But then she stepped from the trees. He swung from the saddle as she came toward him and he was again taken by the handsomeness of her as she studied his face with a poised, contained air.

"I was afraid you might not come back," she said in English and he caught the enjoyment in her face as she saw his surprise.

"Where did you learn my tongue?" he asked.

"One of our people taught me. He learned when he scout for the soldiers," she said. "You have done brave thing for me. Why?"

"Seemed the right thing to do," Fargo said.

"The soldiers were going to kill me," she said.

"They weren't soldiers," he said. She frowned, not understanding. He touched his shirt. "The soldier's clothes, their uniforms, they were masks." She frowned, trying to understand. "Masks," he said and used his hands to illustrate a mask. "As the corn dancers use, as the ghost dancers, the Iroquois False Face Society."

"Yes, yes," she said finally, comprehension coming to her. "Why?"

He turned up his hands as he shrugged. "I do not know. I want to know."

"You save me. Part of my life is yours," she said.

"No, no," he demurred.

"I must give you something back, something very great," she said.

"Don't need anything," he said.

"It is our way. I will find something. You are my warrior," she said.

"No, I'm nobody's warrior. What do they call you?" he asked.

"Little Bird," she said, using sign language to help.

"I'll take you home, Little Bird," he said.

"This way. I could have gone back alone," she said and he frowned in surprise.

"But you waited. Why?"

"It was what I wanted to do," she said with quiet regality as he hurried to follow her.

"Wait, we will ride," he said, taking her arm. She let him help her onto the Ovaro and he felt a slender waist under the elkskin dress, but a lithe, firmly muscled body. He swung onto the horse behind her and she pointed the way for him.

"What do they call you?" she asked.

"Fargo," he said.

She nodded and turned the name in her mind. When they reached the mushroom field she half turned in the saddle, sliding from the Ovaro with a quick, graceful motion. "I go alone now, Fargo. You cannot come with me," she said.

"Why not?" Fargo frowned.

"My father would have you killed," she said.

"Even though I saved his daughter?"

"You would be killed quickly, as a brave warrior is killed."

"Thanks for small favors," Fargo said as she frowned, the remark's meaning passing over her head. "Why does he hate so?" Fargo asked.

"My father is Tall Tree, chief of all the Pawnee," she said and her contained, regal calm was suddenly explained. "To my father, our people have chosen him to destroy all those who come to our lands, soldiers, settlers, everyone. It is his mission, his duty," she said.

"Do you believe in that?" Fargo asked.

"I am not a Pawnee chief. I do not like killing," she said. "By now, my father has heard the soldiers took me. He will not believe they were not real soldiers. He will say you lie for them because they are your people. He will not believe you. Neither will the other chiefs. So you must leave me now."

"There must be a better way to live together. Killing will only bring more killing," Fargo said.

"The Pawnee do not kill alone," she said.

"I know that. There is blame enough all around. More reason for it to stop," Fargo said.

"It will not stop. Too many do not want it to stop," she said. He heard the sadness in her voice and felt unaccountably encouraged by it. She began to walk away and he caught her arm.

"I want to see you again. I want to talk again. Maybe it'll be important," he said.

Her black eyes peered back, her handsome face unsmiling. "Yes, I want that, too."

"Where can I see you?"

"There is a place. I go there often. It is my place to be alone, to talk to the wind and the Great Spirits," she said.

"Tell me."

"Go north. Find the round rock. Go behind it," she said.

"I'll go look for you there. Talk to your father. Make him believe about the soldiers," Fargo said.

She smiled, a rueful smile, but it softened the contained handsomeness of her face, giving it a new beauty. "I will tell him," she said. "And he will tell me I am a child who believes too quickly." She touched his cheek with the back of her hand, a soft touch. "Thank you again, my warrior," she said and hurried away, her back very straight, and he watched her go until she disappeared in the trees. He turned the Ovaro and rode back, cutting east and then north. Though the sun was still shining, he felt as though he rode in shadows as he headed toward the Smoky River.

3

Fargo rode easily under the new morning sun. He had spent the night camped in a thicket of evening primrose, surrounded by their yellow flowers. He had stayed awake wondering again about the six men and the attack on the lovely Indian girl, finally letting sleep push aside what he couldn't explain. When morning came he rose and rode northeast again. He followed Bear Creek to the Arkansas and then turned sharply north. He picked up the end of the Smoky Hill River and followed its banks east, his eyes scouring the prairie. Unshod pony prints were plentiful, crisscrossing each other, some in large clusters of at least twenty horses.

The shadows inside him continued to stay and it was past noon when he came onto the field camp. He was surprised to see how large it was. Rows of tents formed neat patterns along the south bank of the river. Rows of troopers doing various chores took note of him as he rode past and he saw two platoons doing maneuver exercises, peeling off, coming together, executing basic wheel and charge actions. They were not very good, he noted, their timing poor, their execution ragged. He saw a half-dozen Conestogas, men, women, and children beside them, small pup tents set up alongside each. The large tent with the commander's flag flying above it rested nearly at the very end of the camp and he steered the Ovaro toward it.

Dismounting in front of it, two troopers came forward to greet him. "General Davis, soldier," Fargo said. "Skye Fargo calling." One of the troopers hurried inside the tent. Both were terribly young, he noted as he waited. In moments Miles Davis hurried from the tent, his silver hair thick and flowing as always, his ruggedly good-looking face tanned, the smile as welcoming and warm as always.

"Fargo, you old horse thief. God, what a happy surprise," the general boomed as he shook hands. "Come inside, by God, come inside." Fargo followed Miles Davis into a large tent where wooden file cabinets had been set up and wall maps hung on flat bulletin boards. A flap led into another part of the tent, where Fargo glimpsed a cot and a table. The general gestured to one of two straight-backed chairs that faced a small wooden desk. "Sit down and tell me what brings you here." Miles Davis said, his uniform, Fargo saw, as creased and tight-fitting as always.

"Was close enough to visit," Fargo said and drew a skeptical glance.

"What else? Remember, we go back a long ways," the general said.

Fargo allowed a chuckle. "Some questions and some not-so happy news," he said.

"The news first," the general said.

"Pawnee attacks on settlers just west of Bear Creek. I was able to rescue one family and bring in another," Fargo said.

The general's mouth tightened. "Haven't heard about those yet," he said. "But attacks are increasing. I've had a regular patrol out on all the settlements but, as you know, a patrol's a patrol. It's not round-the-clock protection and a lot of the settlements are damn far from one another. But that's only one of my problems."

"Seems you've a bigger force than I've seen," Fargo said.

"It's larger, twenty-five percent larger, and all new," Miles Davis said, and Fargo heard the bitterness in his voice. "They replaced my entire troop, officers and privates. Rotation, they called it," Davis said.

"Whose idea was that?" Fargo asked.

"Official orders came from the Department of the Army. General Herb Cogwell engineered it, I'm certain."

"Cogwell? I met the general when I brought the wagons into Fort Travis. Didn't take to him," Fargo said.

"General Cogwell and I don't see alike on a lot of things," Miles Davis said. "He thinks a hard hand will keep the peace out here. I think it'll set the prairie in a bloodbath. That's why he gave me twenty-five percent more men, he said, and ordered me to set up this field camp."

"How come he gets to call the shots?"

"Because I'm a brigadier general and he's a major general. He's always wanted one command for all of Kansas himself. He's not been able to sell that to the top brass yet but he still wants it. That's another thing we've never agreed on."

"But he did see fit to increase your force twenty-five percent," Fargo said.

"Take a walk with me," Miles Davis said, rising abruptly, and Fargo followed him from the command tent. He fell in beside him as he strode along the tents of the field camp. He walked briskly, waving off hurried salutes as he took Fargo past the troopers engaged in polishing equipment, cleaning rifles, grooming their mounts, shoveling manure, and performing all the chores that were part of cavalry life. Further away, the squads continued their maneuvers. "Look at all these good troopers and tell me what you see, old friend," the general said as he turned and strode back along another line of troops.

Fargo half smiled. His answer had already been formed. "None of them have shaved for very long," he said.

"That's one way to put it. Wet behind the ears is another. They're all practically kids. They gave me a force with minimum training, no real fieldwork, and no combat experience. That doesn't add up to twenty-five percent more men, not against the Indians. It adds up to a hundred percent less."

"Why'd he do it then?" Fargo questioned.

"General Cogwell's smart. He's protecting his flank. He doesn't want to be criticized for the rotation. Twenty-five percent more troops looks good on paper and that's what the top brass will see," Miles Davis said. "Smart and clever."

"Seems so," Fargo agreed.

"But I'm supposed to keep the peace and control the tribes and I don't even have a trooper who can scout Indians. I'm worried, Fargo, real worried. Something's brewing out there," the general said as they returned to the command tent.

"I'll give you something more to chew on," Fargo said and recounted the attack on Little Bird by the six fake troopers. "It was deliberate and planned," Fargo finished. "Aimed at inflaming the Pawnees."

"That has to be Bart Whitman." The general frowned. "Whitman's a gun runner. We know he's been supplying the Pawnee with rifles but we haven't been able to catch him at it."

"Where do the Pawnee get the money to buy rifles?" Fargo questioned.

"They have their kind of money. They exchange fancy pelts with Whitman, the kind that'll bring him more money than the rifles are worth. The more he can stir up the Indians, the more guns they'll want," Davis said.

"And the more they'll use them," Fargo added.

"That's damn sure," the general agreed grimly. "Look, you're here and I need you. I want you to scout for me, ride the territory, read the signs the way only you can read them. Then I want you to work with these kids, teach them how to save their necks and how to fight the Indian. My usual pay, way above scale. You know that."

"Above scale for the army," Fargo said. "You're asking a lot, Miles."

"I know that," the general said. "But it means a lot of settlers will live instead of die, a lot of kids will get a chance to grow up."

"Maybe," Fargo said.

"They'll take that maybe. So will I," Miles Davis said.

"You're always a hard man to refuse," Fargo grumbled.

"Because you've got a conscience," the general said as a figure appeared at the entrance to the tent. Fargo saw a young lieutenant with reddish hair and freckles on a smooth-cheeked face. "This is Lieutenant Horgan," Miles said. "Skye Fargo. Skye will be working with us."

"Glad to meet you, sir," the young officer said with a quick salute.

"Fargo will be training your men in Indian fighting," the general said.

"I'm going to try," Fargo corrected. "You keep up with your formation maneuvers until I get around to you, Lieutenant. Might be a day or two."

"Yes, sir," Horgan said and retreated from the tent. Fargo started for the tent flap, the general following.

"I won't learn anything hanging around here," he said. "This Bart Whitman, what's he look like?"

"Big, fat, about two fifty, jowly face and big belly."

"Where's his base?"

"He keeps shifting it. Last place was a town called Cotton, west of here near the Solomon River."

"If he planned the attack on the chief's daughter he's going to be out looking to supply more guns to the Pawnee. I'll keep an eye peeled for him," Fargo said.

"He's usually got a couple of wagons with him," the general said as Fargo climbed onto the pinto and left with a wave. Riding back along the row of tents, Fargo put the horse into a canter as the sun drifted down toward the horizon line. He had an hour to crisscross the plains before the day came to an end. There were too many Indian pony prints to make him happy. He camped out on the flatland when night came, let sagebrush cluster around him, and ate cold beef jerky, washing it down with good water from his canteen. He listened to the soft scurrying of the deer mice and pocket gophers before he dropped off to sleep.

He rode again when morning came, his eyes scanning the terrain, reading the marks and signs he saw. He slowed, quickly retreating into a stand of box elder when he glimpsed a large knot of horsemen in the distance. Watching from the trees, he saw them draw closer. They passed him and headed northeast. Thirty almost naked bucks, he counted, and his eyes focused on the armband of one. A silent whistle left his lips. No Pawnee, these. Kansa. They rode slowly, casually, and wore no war paint. They were plainly on their way for a rendezvous with the Pawnee. The Kansa were not one of the more warlike tribes, yet they were not above making war. As

Fargo watched them move on, he swore softly. The fact that they were meeting with the Pawnee was disturbing enough. The possible meaning of it was genuinely ominous.

He moved out of the trees and continued to scout the terrain, climbing up onto a low rise for a better view and pausing to focus in on a collection of hoofprints that told him riders had stopped to camp for the night. He rode down to the prints and saw the wagon wheel tracks nearby. They had camped, breakfasted, and gone west, he saw, not toward the Pawnee camp. He decided to follow, nonetheless, and it was past noon when he spotted the two wagons, both Owensboro Kansas-Nebraska wagons with narrow tracks. Both had been outfitted with canvas tops. Six riders rode alongside the wagons and Fargo put the Ovaro into a trot that took him across the front of the first wagon.

He halted and the wagons came to a stop. There was no mistaking Bart Whitman sitting next to the driver of the first wagon, his bulk overflowing on his half of the seat. His face was made of quivering jowls, thick lips, and small eyes. The six riders looked on sullenly. "Bart Whitman, I believe," Fargo said blandly.

"How'd you know?" Whitman frowned.

"General Davis. He told me to watch for you," Fargo said.

"Davis," Whitman said and almost spat out the name. "Why's he botherin' me?"

"He's just interested in you," Fargo said.

"You army?" the man questioned.

"Scouting for the general," Fargo said.

"Same thing," Whitman said.

"Name's Fargo. Mind if I have a look inside your wagons?" Fargo asked.

"Go ahead," Whitman said and Fargo grimaced inwardly at Whitman's ready compliance. The riders pulled back as Fargo went to the first wagon, then the second, moving the canvas back on each to peer inside. Both wagons were filled with pelts, beaver, otter, silver fox, red fox, ermine, and a lot of buffalo hides, all pelts that'd fetch a fancy price on the open market.

"Where'd you get all these?" Fargo asked.

"From my suppliers. Trappers, hunters," Whitman said. Fargo grunted inwardly. He was too late. A lot of rifles had been exchanged. The transaction had already taken place somewhere else at another time. He ran his hand over the pelts. They were warm. They'd been traveling in the wagons a good while. He backed from the wagons and saw the smug satisfaction in Whitman's blubbery face.

"Next time," he said.

"Sure," Whitman said and Fargo watched the two wagons roll on. Eventually they turned and headed west. Something pushed at him as he rode. Whitman was plainly selling guns to the Pawnee. But the attack on Little Bird had nothing to do with this exchange. There hadn't been enough time for all the pieces to be set in motion. If Whitman had been behind the attack, why had he picked a time when he was already in the middle of an exchange with the Pawnee? He wouldn't have had more rifles with him to sell and they probably hadn't more pelts to exchange. It didn't fit. Unless his hired attackers had jumped the gun, Fargo mused. That could explain the bad timing. He turned the explanation over in his mind and decided to live with it until he had something better.

He turned the horse south, his eyes reading the terrain as he rode and finally he drew near the place where Little Bird had left him in the field of mushrooms. He slowed the Ovaro and pushed on across the field through a growth of cottonwoods until they ended and the land grew open with only occasional clusters of black oak. He explored, moving in a zigzag pattern until he spied the round rock Little Bird had named. The day was already moving to an end. He didn't expect to find her but he rode to the rock, a huge sandstone formation, tall and round and polished by wind and weather until it did resemble a huge ball. Moving the horse to the other side, he came upon a small field of green grass and serviceberry and tall, gently waving cerise-lavender blazing stars. It was a restful, serene place indeed fit for talking to the great spirits.

He moved on, across the small field, his eyes peering at the ground until he picked up a set of moccasined footprints. Following, he moved into a dense forest and let his nose and ears be his guide. Little Bird would not have gone too far from the main camp to her place of being alone, he felt certain, and he could see his guess was right when he picked up the odor of campfires. Moving slowly forward, he followed the scent as it grew stronger. The sounds of voices came next and then, halting, he peered forward through the trees, which were mostly bur oak, with their shiny, dense leaves. He glimpsed figures at the perimeter of the camp and didn't dare go closer while the daylight still held. But he saw enough to be able distinguish a full base camp with numerous teepees.

He backed the Ovaro, finally turning the horse when he was out of sight of the camp, and then retreated through the forest. Dusk was beginning to lower when he reached the end of the forest. He started to cross into clear land when he halted and drew back quickly. A band of loin-clothed riders were crossing the open land, some forty of them, Fargo quickly counted. They were obviously on their way to the main Pawnee camp and there was still enough light for Fargo to see the bead-work and designs on gauntlets, cuffs, and parfleches. As his eyes narrowed on the symmetrically bordered decorations, he let the single word fall from his lips silently. Kiowa. Not until they had vanished from sight on their way to the Pawnee main camp did he send the Ovaro forward at a walk. He went into a trot when he reached the round rock and hurried on.

Night fell and he kept going until he came into sight of the Smoky Hill River and the army field camp stretched along its banks. A trooper took his horse after he dismounted in front of the command tent. "Feed him and give him a rubdown," Fargo said. "Much obliged." He strode into the tent as the soldier led the pinto away. General Davis looked at Fargo with wary eyes, his silver white hair glistening in the lamplight.

"You had a long day. Find anything?" the general asked.

"Nothing you're going to like," Fargo said. He told him about meeting Whitman and, more importantly, the appearance of the Kansa and the Kiowa. The general's face had turned ashen by the time he finished.

"It's worse than I feared. They're bringing in other tribes. They're preparing a general uprising," he said.

"What can you do?" Fargo asked.

"With the crew I have? Not a lot. I wouldn't dare try an attack. But I can't just sit and wait. I'll double my patrols. That'll be the first thing, let them know we can raise the stakes, too."

"But it'll be a bluff," Fargo said.

"They don't know that. I'll be buying time," Davis said.

"You'll be riding on damn thin ice," Fargo said. "If we can stop them from getting another big batch of rifles it might make them back off some. That means getting

46

Whitman. After the attack on his daughter, Tall Tree will want every rifle he can get. He'll be contacting Whitman. Where? The man must operate from someplace."

"He's tricky. He has no base. He keeps on the move, lets only the Pawnee know where to reach him."

"I'll get a few hours' sleep and head out again. Maybe I can be there when the Pawnee meet him. It's worth a try," Fargo said.

"Anything's worth a try. You want a platoon to go with you?"

"Not now. I'd never find Whitman with a platoon," Fargo said and he left the general staring into space. He found an adjoining tent and stretched out on the cot. Tiredness brought sleep quickly. When he woke to his own inner clock, he sat up, the night still dark, and used a water basin to freshen up before getting the Ovaro. The night sky told him dawn was still hours away as he rode past sentries and left the field camp. Using the moon and the stars as guideposts, he held a steady pace westward but slowed down before the moon dipped below the horizon.

In the deep dark before dawn, he drew to a halt at the edge of the burr oaks that hid the Pawnee camp, dismounted, and sat down until the soft gray of the new day began to dissipate the night. The forest took shape as dawn rose and Fargo stayed hidden in the trees, peering out at the main part of the forest. He waited beside the Ovaro and hoped he had guessed right. It turned out not to be a long wait. The first edge of the sun had just touched the trees when the lone Pawnee rider streaked into view, crossing into open land, riding hard on his short-legged pony. Fargo let him go, almost out of sight, before he climbed onto the Ovaro and set out after the Indian pony. He stayed back, making certain he wouldn't be seen, though the rider was plainly concentrating on making time. Taking a path into low hills, he was able to keep the Pawnee in sight and draw closer.

When, after the sun had crossed the noon sky the rider turned south to race alongside a thick stand of staghorn sumac, Fargo had to abandon the hills and fall in behind the rider again. At the sumac, he entered the trees, slowing as he saw the Pawnee turn into the woods. The Indian moved through the trees for another ten minutes until the small clearing suddenly appeared. Fargo reined to a halt when he saw the two wagons, the figures lounging alongside. Bart Whitman's fat bulk was immediately recognizable as it came forward to meet the messenger. Too far away to hear clearly, Fargo managed to pick up the stern urgency in the Indian's voice. Plainly a courier carrying orders, the Pawnee gesticulated as he spoke, his actions and tone clearly demanding.

After he finished delivering his message, he climbed onto his sturdy quarter horse and rode away. Fargo stayed in the sumac, letting the rider disappear as he watched Bart Whitman. As the others picked up their gear and saddled their horses, Whitman pulled his bulk into the first wagon. When his driver joined him, he ordered the wagons forward. The Pawnee order had been given by the courier. Now Whitman was going to fill it. General Davis was right about the man. Whitman was cagey, plainly keeping his cache of weapons hidden away, undoubtedly scattered in more than one place. Fargo slowly moved the Ovaro forward as the wagons rolled out of the sumac and onto open land. When he glanced at the sun, he saw it was already moving down toward the horizon. Whitman wouldn't keep the rifles close or easy for someone to find. It would be night before he'd reach them, Fargo was certain, and then he'd have to load the wagons. It'd be the next day before he'd be ready to rendezvous with the Pawnee again.

Turning, Fargo broke off trailing the wagons. Following Whitman wasn't important. Catching him with the rifles was and he'd need help for that, Fargo decided. He sent the Ovaro down a long slope as the day began to fade, and began the long ride back to Smoky Hill River. Night descended before he followed its path west. It was approaching midnight when he reached the field camp. He waited for the sentries to pass him through and wake the general. Miles Davis greeted him in a blue army robe and listened in silence until he finished. "But you don't know where he'll be meeting the Pawnee with the rifles. There's a hell of a lot of prairie," the general said.

"I've narrowed it down. The Pawnee have picked the place. They won't meet too close to their camp but they won't travel all over creation, either. I'm pretty sure of the general area they'll choose. If I'm there come dawn, I'll find Whitman first, before he meets with the Pawnee," Fargo said.

"You'll need troops, at least twenty. I'll send Horgan with Troop B," the general said.

"Have them ready to ride in four hours," Fargo said.

"I'll see to it myself," Davis said and once again Fargo found a cot and got in a few hours' sleep while the Ovaro was fed and rubbed down. The night was still deep and dark when he was in the saddle again, Lieutenant Horgan's young freckled face riding beside him, the rhythmic clip-clop of the platoon at his back. He led the way through the remainder of the night and when the first gray-pink streaks of dawn touched the earth, his eyes were as an eagle's sweeping the terrain. He had made a reasoned guess and was still confident that he was not far off the mark. His confidence was rewarded an hour later when the two wagons came into sight. He recognized them at once as Whitman's Kansas-Nebraska rigs outfitted with the canvas tops. A driver guided each with four riders alongside.

"Company in twos," Lieutenant Horgan called to his platoon. "Close in from both sides." Fargo peered hard at the two wagons as he closed in on them and felt the furrow dig into his brow. The furrow deepened as he neared the wagons and saw them come to a halt. "Ah, shit," he bit out and drew a glance from Horgan. "Whitman's not with them," Fargo muttered, reaching the wagons and drawing to a halt. He glared at the driver of the first wagon. "Where is he?" Fargo snapped.

"He went off someplace. I don't know where," the driver said.

"That's a lie," Fargo snapped.

"He didn't tell me," the man insisted sullenly.

"We'll be having a look at those wagons," Lieutenant Horgan said and motioned to his men.

"The rifles aren't there, dammit," Fargo said and heard the bitter frustration in his voice.

"They could be. Examine the wagons," Horgan ordered and eight of the troopers dismounted, four going to each wagon.

"They're empty," Fargo said impatiently.

"No rifles, sir," one of the troopers called.

"None here, either," the soldiers said from the second wagon.

"Take up the floorboards. They could be hidden underneath," Horgan said.

"They're not there, dammit," Fargo burst out. "He sent these for us to find. They're goddamn decoys. You're wasting time."

"I can't go without a proper search," the lieutenant said. "That'd be against proper procedures."

"Shit," Fargo said and wheeled the Ovaro in a tight circle. "You go ahead. When you've finished, ride north and look for me." He sent the pinto into a gallop and swore at the lieutenant's military preoccupation with proper procedures. He also swore at Whitman's cleverness. But one thing still held. Whitman was meeting with the Pawnee somewhere not too far away, and Fargo's eyes searched the plains as he rode in a zigzag pattern.

When he spotted a long line of bur oak he raced the horse toward the trees, rode into the edge of the treeline, and followed the forest north. He'd gone perhaps another fifteen minutes when he spied the two wagons tight alongside the edge of the oak, virtually invisible from the center of the plains. He pushed the Ovaro through the trees, slowing only when he saw the knot of figures, some on foot, some on their ponies. He swung from the saddle, dropped the reins over a low branch, and crept forward on foot.

He spotted Bart Whitman's big bulk at once, the man standing near the tailgate of one of the wagons. The Pawnee facing him wore a beaded vest, leggings, and a lone eagle's feather in his hair. But it was his build that held Fargo's eyes, at least six feet three inches in height, ramrod straight, a face as severe as a tamarack. Tall Tree, Fargo thought to himself and recognized the Pawnee beside him as the courier who now served as interpreter. Fargo crept close enough to hear, staying hidden in the foliage as he listened. He heard the tone of dissension before he caught the words. "Chief say we need more time to gather skins but need rifles now. We pay you many skins later," the interpreter said.

"No skins no rifles," Whitman said truculently. "That's the deal, same as always."

The courier answered after a quick exchange with

Tall Tree. "Chief say this is not same, need rifles now. Skins will come," he translated.

Whitman's fat face looked back with skeptical annoyance. "No skins no guns, dammit," he said.

The chief spit out words and the courier spoke. "You have word of Chief of Pawnee," he said and Fargo's eyes flicked to the tall, ramrod-straight figure and saw icy pride in the stern, spare face.

"I'll bring the guns back when he gets the skins," Whitman said. He was impugning the chief's word, the greatest of all insults. Fargo groaned silently. He was on dangerous ground. But he was essentially a stupid, greedy man. There was a moment of terrible silence that Whitman was too crass to grasp. "Come see me when you're ready," he growled and started to turn to the wagon.

Fargo saw the fury in the chief's eyes as he brought his hand up and then down in a short, chopping motion. The surrounding Pawnee warriors erupted, a hail of arrows and bullets filling the air. Whitman's men beside the wagons went down almost as one. Whitman's big bulk slowly sank to the ground, quivering and shuddering, not unlike a huge bowl of pudding, before finally lying still. It had all taken but seconds and Fargo watched the Pawnee descend on the wagons with triumphant war whoops as they gathered up bundles of rifles, most of them good army carbines, Fargo noted, with a few Winchesters added. He stayed silent and watched the Pawnee ride away carrying the rifles, the tall, straight figure at the front. He moved only when they were out of sight, returning to where he'd left the Ovaro and riding in the other direction.

When he emerged onto the open land, he stayed at a trot for perhaps another five minutes until he spied the line of troops coming toward him at a full gallop. He halted, let them come to a stop. Horgan was in the lead. "You were right. There were no rifles," the lieutenant said.

"Thanks," Fargo said laconically. Horgan had the manners to look sheepish.

"You find Whitman?" Horgan asked.

"Oh yes." Fargo nodded mildly.

"He sell his rifles?"

"Not exactly, but the Pawnee have them now," Fargo said, explaining what had happened in flat sentences that needed no embellishment. "He could have kept his scalp if he weren't so goddamn dumb," Fargo added. "Let's get back." He turned the Ovaro and the troop fell into line behind him as the lieutenant rode at his side. He rode at a brisk trot, grateful for Horgan's silence, yet it was dark by the time they reached the field camp, where the general listened in stony silence. He rose when Fargo finished, his face suddenly old.

"How much time do we have before they explode? That's the only thing that matters, now," he said.

"I might be able to get an idea," Fargo said.

"Anything you can find out will help," the general said.

"Something bothers me about what happened. You feel Whitman was stirring up the Pawnee to sell rifles. You think he was behind the six fake troopers' attack on the chief's daughter," Fargo said and the general nodded. "If he was that clever, how come he was so stupid with the Pawnee?"

"Men make mistakes," the general shrugged.

"That wasn't a mistake. That was a man too stupid to understand the people he was dealing with," Fargo said.

"What are you saying?" Davis asked.

"Don't rightly know, only that something doesn't fit,"

Fargo said. "I'll think more on it." The general nodded and Fargo walked from the tent, found the empty pup tent nearby, and stretched out on the cot. He slept quickly, but it was a restless sleep made of ugly shadows and hanging questions.

4

Fargo rode through the new day with his eyes constantly
scanning the ground. He avoided a dozen Pawnee riders
and continued to move north. It was midafternoon when
he passed the round rock and walked the horse forward
through the cerise-lavender blazing stars. He had almost
reached the last of the flowers when she stepped into
sight. He halted and swung from the saddle. He watched
her come closer, the elkskin dress tied at the waist with a
thin, rawhide string that outlined the slenderness of her
body. He was struck again by the handsomeness of her
even-featured face, her jet hair hanging loosely and soft-
ening the somewhat austere regality of her face.

"I wondered if you would come," Little Bird said,
halting only inches from him, her black, liquid eyes
searching his face. "I waited each day."

"I am honored," Fargo said.

Her hand touched his arm, a warm, soft pressure. She
smelled of honeysuckle, a scent both sweet and provoca-
tive. "I hoped you would come," she said, letting a tiny
smile edge her lips. "Do I surprise you?"

"Maybe," he allowed.

"There is no need for childish games between us," she
said.

"No?" he said.

"You saved me. We have a special bond. It is the way

of my people." She drew him down on the soft grass beside her as she sat cross-legged. The black, liquid eyes peered at him, studying him and a smile touched her lips, edged with rue. "But you did not come just to see me," she said.

"I would have. I will," he said, stumbling and feeling clumsy. Her simple, straight directness was as unsettling as the shimmering handsomeness of her. "Your father has many new rifles," he said. "Will he use them now? Will he make the prairies run red?"

"Not yet," Little Bird said. Fargo felt hope leap inside him. The explosion was not imminent. Good news and he embraced it quickly.

"Your father waits because he thinks again of what this will mean to his people?" Fargo suggested.

"He waits because there are others coming. The Osage and the Cheyenne are sending warriors," Little Bird said. Fargo cursed silently. The good news was suddenly not at all good. He took Little Bird by the shoulders.

"It is no good. It will bring only terrible things. Tell him we can find another way. Make him listen," Fargo implored.

"He will not listen to me. Too many others fill his ears with talk of killing," she said, reaching up and laying her hand against his face. "Let us not talk of this. Let us talk of you and I."

"We will. I will come back. I promise," he said and used sign language to emphasize his words. She searched his face for another moment, then leaned forward and rested her cheek against his.

"It is meant to be," she said. "I will wait. It is for me to wait."

"It's for you to help find a way to stop the killing. That first, then us," he said.

"Can you stop the wind from blowing? You can do only what is given you to do," she said.

"We'll do more," he said, trying to reach beyond the fatalism that was part of her. He moved suddenly and pressed his mouth to hers, letting the warm strength of his lips push at her. It took a moment but he felt her mouth open. A sharp gasp came from her, and when he pulled back, the liquid eyes stared at him. "Remember this till I come back," he said. "Find a way to reach your father. Do them both for me." She didn't reply but her eyes were grave as they followed him to where he climbed onto the Ovaro. He blew a kiss to her as he rode away and wondered if he'd found a way to her.

She was a strange mixture, a chief's daughter full of the ways of her people, committed to ancient customs, regal, contained but wide-eyed, almost timid, and unable to go beyond the boundaries of her world. Perhaps he had given her new reasons to do so, he hoped as he rode west. He stayed close to tree lines as much as he could, again avoiding bands of Pawnee horsemen moving across the plains. Near the Smoky Hills, he took a rise in the land and rode along a ledge where he could look down on the land below. He saw three ledges paralleling each other, the one just below where he rode well covered with shadbush. His eyes dropped down to the next ledge and the frown came to his brow. A lone rider moved slowly along the ledge and Fargo caught the sun as it glinted on light brown, shoulder-length hair and a yellow blouse. The young woman leaned forward in the saddle and peered down to the third, bottom ledge. Fargo saw what she watched, a party of six Pawnee braves moving single file.

Staying back from the edge of the flat ledge, the young woman kept to the back of the ledge to stay out of sight. She had to lean far out of the saddle to watch the line of Pawnee below her and she slowed almost to a halt and let the Indians move on. What in hell was she doing out here alone, Fargo wondered. She stopped and waited, her eyes on the Pawnee below as they rode on. The movement caught the corner of his eye and he glanced to his right, where the loin-clothed figure crouched under one of the shadbush. The Indian watched the watcher, his focus concentrated on the young woman, his pony tied under a nearby shadbush. Staying in a crouch, he moved forward to the edge of the ledge and began to position himself just above the young woman. She was still absorbed in watching the line of Pawnee ride off, totally unaware of the figure poised just above her.

Fargo slid from the saddle. Pausing to take the lariat from its strap, he landed on the tips of his toes. There was no question about what was about to unfold in front of him and there was no question that he couldn't use his Colt. A shot would bring the line of Pawnee charging back at once. They were still well within hearing range. The lone Pawnee was letting himself slide a few yards down toward the ledge where the young woman waited and watched.

Fargo echoed the Pawnee and let himself slide a few yards down toward the ledge below. He stopped his slide as he saw the near-naked figure halt, rise up on his haunches, and leap. Lithe as a cougar, the Pawnee timed his leap perfectly, landing on the young woman. His arms were already wrapped around her as she toppled sideways from the saddle and was atop her when she hit the ground. He pulled her onto her back instantly and yanked the yellow blouse over her head, stifling any cries. Straddling her, he began to pull the top of her slip off. He was plainly not about to share her with the others until he'd enjoyed her for himself. Fargo had the lariat uncoiled and sent it whirling through the air. When it landed over the Pawnee's head, the Indian glanced up in surprise. Fargo yanked hard, the noose instantly tightening around the man's neck. The Pawnee clutched at the rope around his neck with both hands as he fell from the girl. But Fargo pulled harder and he rolled, his legs kicking out furiously.

The noose already shutting off his breath, the Pawnee stopped trying to pull it free from his neck. He reached down to his belt and pulled up a hunting knife. With his remaining strength, he began to cut at the taut part of the lariat. There wasn't time to get down to him, Fargo saw. Drawing the thin double-edged throwing knife from his calf holster, he took a moment to aim and send the blade hurtling downward with all his strength. The Pawnee had already cut the lariat almost in half when the blade slammed through the side of his neck, imbedding itself to the hilt. The Pawnee stiffened instantly, stayed that way for a brief moment, and then went limp, his arms and legs finally letting go with a final twitch.

Fargo was already sliding down to the second ledge, and then the third, where the young woman sat. She had pulled the yellow blouse down from over her head and scooted back a few paces, but her eyes were still round with shock and fright. He came down on the lowest ledge and went to her. She was clinging to him instantly. "Oh my God, oh my God," she said and he felt the trembling of her. He held her until the trembling stopped and he pulled back to look at her. The first fright had left her and he saw an attractive young woman, her light brown hair worn loose yet neat, her eyes a matching light brown with thinly arched brows. Nicely formed lips were still slightly parted, her cheekbones high yet not really pronounced. The blouse rested on modest breasts, and as he rose and pulled her to her feet he saw that she was tall, with a long waist and a sinewy figure. "I was being so careful, watching everything," she said.

"You have to learn how to watch Indians," he said. "You can't assume that the ones you see are the only ones there."

"Obviously not," she said with a tiny shudder.

"They often have an outrider. They believe in being careful, no surprises," Fargo said. The young woman's light brown eyes were almost hazel, he noted as she peered at him. She came forward, her arms going around his neck as she held on to him.

"Thank God you were there. I don't have enough words to thank you," she said, lifting her head to look deeply at him.

"Glad I was here," he said. "Name's Fargo . . . Skye Fargo."

"Well, Skye Fargo, thank God you were riding this way," she said.

"Would you like to tell me what in hell you're doing out here alone?"

"I'm trying to get to Fort Travis," she answered.

"Your timing is damn bad," Fargo said. "This territory is close to exploding. The tribes are ready to hit the warpath. I'm surprised you got this far."

"I've got to go on. Can you take me to Fort Travis? I've some money. I'll pay you," the young woman said.

"Money's no matter. I'm not sure I could get you there in one piece and I've other things to do," Fargo said. "There's an army field camp closer. I'd have a better chance of getting you there."

"No, no other army post. I want to get to Fort Travis. I have to see General Cogwell," she said and he heard the determination come into her tone.

"That so important?"

"Yes. The general's my father. I'm Caryn Cogwell," she said and Fargo let a low whistle escape his lips.

"Does he know you're coming?" he asked.

"No. I'm going to surprise him," Caryn Cogwell said.

"You sure as hell are," Fargo said.

"Good," Caryn Cogwell snapped. "That's exactly what I want to do."

He regarded her for a moment, surprised by the coldness in her voice. She let her almost hazel eyes soften. "Please take me, Fargo. I know I've no right to ask anything more of you after what you've done but I've nowhere else to turn."

"What if I said no, it's too dangerous?" he countered.

"I'd go on alone. I came a long way and it'd be just as dangerous to turn back," Caryn Cogwell said, stiffening.

She was right about that much. "Guess I'm stuck with you," he muttered.

"That's something less than gracious," Caryn said.

"I'm something less than gracious with people who do damn fool things," he tossed back.

"Is that what I've done?" she asked.

"What would you call it?" he challenged. "Even without the territory being on fire, this is dangerous land, no place for a woman to be riding alone."

"I had to come. I guess I didn't think enough," she said. "I'm sorry." He glared at her for a moment, then let his face soften. She wasn't the first to underestimate the wildness of the land and she wouldn't be the last.

"I'll try my best. No promises," he said and she threw her arms around him.

"Thank you, Fargo, again," she said as he felt the soft warmth of her before she pulled back.

"Get your horse," he said and climbed back up the slope to the ledge where he'd left the Ovaro. When he was in the saddle he looked down to where she sat a brown gelding. "Stay at a walk," he called to her. "We'll hook up a ways on." He rode forward slowly, keeping her in his vision as he scanned the land ahead. The Pawnee had gone their way and the ledge finally dipped downward to join the ledges below, and Caryn came alongside him. She sat her horse well, her long-waisted figure one with her mount. She had tucked the yellow blouse back into her skirt, and it had tightened around breasts perhaps not as modest as he'd first thought.

A wind blew up and sent sagebrush rolling across their path. There was not a lot of the day left and he stayed north, finally coming to where a half-dozen cabins were stretched out a quarter mile from each other. Farmland reached out beyond each, some with hogs and cattle. He also saw a long line of hoofprints, perhaps twenty horses, he estimated. Caryn's eyes took on alarm as she saw the prints. "One of the general's patrols," he told her. "Horses all wearing shoes, riding in a neat column of twos at a steady pace. Relax." She let a small sigh of relief escape her lips and his eyes went to the cabins as they rode past. He drew a friendly wave from a few of the figures in the fields. "Let's hope we can keep them all looking so peaceful," he murmured and put the pinto into a trot.

He rode on, only slowing when a dust cloud rose in front of them. Eyes narrowed, he studied the cloud as he wheeled the pinto around and led the way into a forest of box elder. Caryn beside him, he sat silently and soon the line of riders appeared. Some fifteen, he guessed, crossed in front of the trees and went their way. "Pawnee," he murmured to Caryn as the Indians receded.

"How'd you know?" she queried.

"You'd be surprised what a dust cloud can tell you," he said. "They're as individual as a cry or a trail. They have their own shape, speed, and movement. An army patrol sends up an entirely different dust spiral than a band of Indians. Riders in a loose bunch give off a very different cloud than riders in a column. The density, the character of the edges, the way the cloud spirals, it all makes a difference."

"Amazing," she murmured as he moved from the trees but stayed along the edge of the forest as he turned south. When night came, he turned back into the trees. He halted when he reached a small clearing.

"We'll bed down here," he said as he unsaddled the Ovaro. The night descended to turn the forest almost pitch black. Caryn had a supply of dried beef and she offered him some. She sat down next to him, the yellow blouse ghostly pale in the darkness. "Maybe you'd like to tell me why it's so important you get to your pa," he suggested between bites.

"I owe you that," she said thoughtfully.

"I'd say so," he agreed.

"But it'll have to wait," she finished crisply.

"You always change off that fast?" He frowned, annoyed.

"I promised myself not to talk about it till I got there. I won't change now, even for you," she said.

"Your show," he conceded and rose to get his bedroll. After setting it out, he began to undress. "We'll be riding early," he said and she rose to change. He undressed to his underwear, stretched out in the warm night, and listened to Caryn in the deep darkness. She materialized at his side wearing what appeared to be a loose, billowy nightdress. She put her blanket almost over the edge of his bedroll and settled down close beside him.

"You're my good-luck coin, Fargo," she said. "You know what you do with a good-luck coin?"

"Never had one. Tell me," he said.

"You keep it close to you," she said, stretched out, and

he felt her hand find his, fingers curling around his. "Good night, Fargo," she murmured and was asleep in minutes. He smiled at the way her hand stayed tight around him. He found himself wondering about her. She plainly had a purpose. Something was pushing hard at her, fueling her single-minded determination. But somehow, he didn't get the feeling her desperate desire to see her father was made of love. There was no warmth in her voice when she spoke of the general, no softness at all. And no coyness to her, no pretense. She was direct, even in refusing an answer, and he liked that. Maybe her tongue would loosen some along the way, he decided as he closed his eyes and let sleep come to him. He liked the feel of her hand in his.

Dawn was just starting to push aside the night when he woke and sat up. Caryn Cogwell lay on her side against him, the billowy nightdress bunched up enough to reveal a long, slender calf. She woke as he rose. Blinking herself into focusing on him, her eyes lingered on his muscled torso. He pulled on clothes and pulled her up with one hand. "Get dressed. I want to make some time while the morning's still new," he said. She went into the trees, changed, and returned in the yellow blouse, brushing her hair as she did. He had the horses saddled and she pulled herself onto the brown gelding and followed him as he moved from the clearing at once.

"You don't give a person a chance to wake up," she grumbled.

"I'm giving you a chance to keep your scalp," he said as he set the Ovaro into a fast canter across open land. It wasn't until the sun rose to bathe the plains that he turned and rode into a stand of black oak. Inside the woods, he found a stream and reined to a halt. "You can wash up here," he said, dismounting and pulling off his clothes. He stepped into the stream, washed, and felt her quick glances as she undressed behind the gelding. When he finished, using a towel from his saddlebag to dry, he called to her. "Your turn," he said.

"I'm not putting on an exhibition," Caryn Cogwell said.

"What's good for the gander is good for the goose," he said.

"You weren't supposed to notice," she said sheepishly. He didn't answer. "Please," she said.

"This one time," he said. He turned away and walked to the edge of the trees, where he searched the plains as she stepped into the stream. His eyes narrowed as, in the distance, he watched two lines of Pawnee racing back and forth, indulging in their own war exercises. Once more, the climate of impending death rolled across the plains, so real one could almost taste it. As the riders finally moved on, Fargo returned to the stream, where Caryn waited, dressed and ready to ride. "We won't be making time. We'll be staying in tree cover," he said and led the way through the box elder. When they had to cross open land he rode ahead and Caryn followed at his sign. It was slow, careful riding, with redmen always too near to take chances, and the day began to slide toward an end when they neared the fort and night descended as they arrived at the line of cabins and tents outside the stockade walls. He glanced at Caryn as they entered the stockade and he saw the tightness in her face. He dismounted with her as she faced the corporal outside the commander's quarters.

"Tell the general his daughter is here," she said. The trooper's eyes widened as he hurried into the building. Fargo waited a few feet from her and in moments General Herbert Cogwell rushed from his quarters. He halted and stood staring at Caryn as if he were seeing a ghost.

"By God," he muttered. "By God. You, it's really you."

"In the flesh," she said.

Cogwell frowned as he continued to stare at her. "How did you get here?" he asked.

"I almost didn't," Caryn said. "Fargo helped me to make it."

Cogwell's eyes flicked to Fargo, a quick, harsh glare, and instantly returned to Caryn. "What are you doing here?" the general rasped at her.

"Aren't you going to tell me how happy you are to see me?" Caryn asked, sarcastic sweetness coating each word.

"Come inside," the general snapped. He spun on his heel and strode into his quarters.

"I'll be leaving you now," Fargo said to Caryn.

"No," she said sharply. "Come with me." She walked into the building and Fargo followed, feeling distinctly ill at ease. He almost welcomed Cogwell's peremptory command.

"I want to speak to Caryn alone," the general said.

"Wait for me," Caryn tossed at him as Fargo walked from the room, halting in the small entranceway.

"You've your goddamn nerve coming here," he heard Cogwell say to Caryn as he pushed the door shut. Through the closed door he could only make out snatches of their conversation, the parts when their voices were raised in angry shouts. "You're leaving here tomorrow," he heard Cogwell say.

"No, I'm not. I'm staying till you agree," Caryn said.

"You're going and I'm not agreeing to anything," the general shouted.

"Then everybody in this camp is going to know about you," Caryn's voice answered.

"Little bitch," Cogwell's shout followed, then the

slam of a fist upon a desk. His next words were muffled, delivered in a tight monotone. Caryn's voice followed, equally muffled, and the bitter exchanges continued until the door was flung open and Caryn stalked out. She came to him, took his arm as she pulled him along, and halted outside in the courtyard of the fort.

"Thanks for waiting," she said.

"You going to be all right?" Fargo asked.

"Yes. I'm not the one afraid," Caryn said defiantly.

"I don't know if he's afraid but Daddy's damn mad," Fargo said.

"Daddy," she said with a snort, the word dipped in venom. "Daddy's a complete bastard, a fraud, a no-good, selfish, unprincipled, rotten excuse for an officer and a gentleman. It sounds terrible to say about your father, doesn't it?" He gave a half shrug, unable to find the right words. "For years, he's been supposed to pay my mother alimony and child support. He's never paid a cent, never sent a dime. He's used all his power and all his connections to avoid his obligations. All he cared about was his own ambitions. Now, Ma is sick and desperate. She needs help and I've come to make him pay up."

"Exactly how do you figure to do that?" Fargo asked, not ungently.

"I'll shame him into it. There are lots of enlisted men and officers' wives here with families, plenty of settlers too. I'll tell everyone the truth about him. He won't want that. The big general won't want the world to know him for what he is. His friends in the army and Washington have helped him keep his secrets. I'm going to put an end to that. He'll pay up to keep me quiet."

"Hope you can do it. You've plainly given a lot of thought to this," Fargo said.

"I'll do it," Caryn said, firm confidence in her voice. Fargo turned as the interruption strode toward them,

General Cogwell's straight, ramrod figure stamping the ground, his face a stern and officious mask.

"Want to talk to you, Fargo," the general snapped. "You helped her get here, you can take her out of here come morning. I want you to deliver her to the stage depot at Cheyenne Wells."

"That'd mean going through the heart of Pawnee country." Fargo frowned.

"You can do it. You're the Trailsman," Cogwell said with something close to a sneer.

"That's right but I'm not invisible," Fargo said.

"Extra bonus pay. That ought to satisfy you," Cogwell said.

"Extra pay doesn't buy a new scalp," Fargo said. "Besides, I'm on assignment to General Davis. I've delayed things by bringing Caryn here."

"Assignment to Davis? I'm countermanding that. You'll obey my orders," Cogwell said.

"You can't do that," Fargo said and saw Cogwell's face darken. "I'm not in the army. I don't take orders. I work for who I want, when I want, and how I want and I'm working for General Davis."

Cogwell's face twitched in fury. "Then leave. You're *persona non grata* in my fort," the general said. "If you know what that means," he added snidely.

Fargo smiled. "It means you're not happy if you don't get your way," he said and the general spun and strode away. Fargo brought his eyes to Caryn. She held her long-waisted figure ramrod straight. "I'm worried about you," he said.

"Don't be. I'll be fine. I'm glad you turned him down. He won't dare bully me in front of the whole fort," Caryn said.

"I'll have to be on my way," Fargo said.

"I know. I didn't expect you to stay," she said. Her

arms rose and encircled his neck and her lips came to his, soft and warm and sweetly moist. "That's for everything. Maybe there'll be a better time," she said.

"I'll arrange that if I can," Fargo said.

"I'd like that," she said, kissed him again, and stepped back. She watched him climb onto the Ovaro and ride off with a wave. Outside the fort he passed the sleeping settlements and rode till the moon was high. He bedded down underneath a pair of wide-branched cottonwoods. If Miles Davis could somehow keep the lid on things, he'd pay another visit to Caryn, he promised himself. Her long-waisted figure lingered in his mind as he drifted off to sleep.

5

Fargo rode north with the new day and cursed as he'd only gone a few miles when a band of exuberant bucks made him take refuge in a formation of pedestal rocks. He went on after they'd gone only to have to scurry into hiding again, this time in a cluster of bur oak, as some twenty Pawnee appeared. As he peered out from inside the trees, he saw that they were plainly searching for targets. They moved in a long circle with lookouts riding ahead to sweep the terrain both east and west. Finally, they shifted directions and moved unhurriedly south. He left the trees and made a careful detour south before riding east again.

The land seemed a waiting place filled with shadows unseen yet very much there. He had seen no sign of a platoon from Miles and he knew there were two good reasons and he approved of both. First, Miles wouldn't order scouting expeditions that could find his inexperienced troops tangling with the Pawnee. Second, he'd keep his platoons patrolling the settlers' cabins. He had little choice for the moment. Miles Davis was like a man trying to keep a pot from boiling over with someone else feeding the fire. Riding carefully, Fargo found himself under a noon sun, scanning the unshod pony prints of Indian horsemen when he spotted a small dust cloud moving toward him. He edged the pinto toward a stand of low-branched serviceberry and frowned. The cloud stayed small, with no definable character, and a frown crossed his brow as the cloud became horsemen, six blue-clad cavalry troopers surrounding a wagon.

Fargo moved from the serviceberry and approached the riders who surrounded the wagon. The frown deepened as he studied the wagon. Square and high, entirely closed except for a small barred window on each side, he recognized it as a delivery wagon that had been converted to a prison van. The young blond face of Lieutenant Roswall rode a half-dozen feet in front of the van and the five troopers that rode alongside and behind it. He raised an arm and brought the little knot of riders to a halt as Fargo came up. An extra trooper drove the van, his mount tied behind, Fargo noted.

Fargo let his eyes scan the troopers, then focused on Lieutenant Roswall. "You looking to get scalped, Lieutenant?" he asked.

"No, sir," the lieutenant said.

"Then I hope you've a dozen riflemen hiding inside that van," Fargo said.

"No, sir," the lieutenant said.

"Then what in hell are you doing out here with that van?" Fargo asked.

The lieutenant was having trouble keeping his face impassive, Fargo noted. "General's orders," he said.

"What's in the van, soldier?" Fargo questioned, his voice growing hard.

Roswall looked uncomfortable. "Not what, sir. Who," he said.

Fargo felt the frown dig into his brow. He swung from the saddle and stepped to the van. When he pulled the door open, he felt the sharp intake of breath rush from his lips. "Goddamn," he swore as Caryn stared back from the flat bench seat, her eyes widening as she saw him.

"Fargo, oh thank God," she gasped. She started to come forward but was stopped by the ankle chain around her left leg attached to a pin inside the wagon. Fargo's eyes went to Roswall.

"You want to explain this?" he barked.

Roswall swallowed hard. "Yes, sir. We're taking Miss Cogwell to the stage depot at Cheyenne Wells."

"In ankle chains? As a prisoner?" Fargo shot back.

"General's orders," the lieutenant said and had the decency to look uncomfortable. Thoughts were racing through Fargo's mind, almost too terrible to entertain. He wanted to turn away from them, deny them, but he couldn't. They burned inside him, an obscene, twisted truth. His eyes stayed on the lieutenant. "I want you to come with me," he said. "But first have your men take the van into the serviceberry, unchain Miss Cogwell, and stay there."

The lieutenant hesitated, but only for a moment. "Do it," he ordered his troopers and Fargo climbed back into the saddle. He waited till the van was out of sight in the tree cover before turning to the lieutenant.

"Do you know what you've been asked to do, Lieutenant?" he asked.

"Take the general's daughter to Cheyenne Wells," Roswall answered.

"No. You've been asked to take her to be killed," Fargo said and the lieutenant stared back. "The general wants to get rid of his daughter and he's cleverly found the perfect way to do it with no questions asked now or later. She's going to be killed in a Pawnee attack, a completely believable happening. Only he's arranged to be sure it happens." He paused. The young

72

officer continued to stare at him, plainly unable to know what to think. "Hard to believe, isn't it, soldier?" he said.

"Yes, sir, it is," Roswall said.

"But not that hard. You've had to be wondering, all of you, six men being sent out here through the heart of the Pawnee country. No limited patrols not far from the fort, this time. You're going straight into the cannon's mouth. You won't have a chance of getting through to Cheyenne Wells with that van and he knows it."

"You're saying he's willing to have his daughter killed. That's bad enough, and he's sacrificing us to do it," Roswall said.

"Bull's-eye, soldier. Oh, he might even hope you'd be able to make a run for it and get away. He's not interested in your dying. But he knows the van will never get away," Fargo said and saw the shock in Roswall's face as the enormity of it sank deeper into him. "Come with me," Fargo said and the lieutenant followed as he moved north. He pointed out a line of unshod pony tracks and went on to point out another and moved further to gesture to a large band of prints. "They're all over the territory. I'd guess they'd spot you within an hour," Fargo said and turned the pinto around as Roswall followed in silence. But the shock was stark in his young face. He could no longer turn away from the unthinkable. It all fitted, too perfectly.

Fargo didn't speak again until they returned to the serviceberry. "Let Caryn go. I'm taking her with me," he said.

"What am I supposed to tell General Cogwell?" Roswall asked.

"Tell him the Pawnee attacked. You got away but they took the wagon. He won't probe. It's what he expects, what he wants," Fargo answered. The lieutenant wrestled with himself, his young face drained. "You wondering about your men?" Fargo asked.

"A little," Roswall said.

"They won't talk. They'll know you're saving their scalps. They've got to be scared riding out here," Fargo said.

"They are. They've said so."

"Then they'll be happy to get back alive. They won't talk," Fargo said.

The lieutenant half shrugged, resignation in his voice. "It could be my career," he said.

"Don't think so, but I know one thing for sure. Dead men don't have careers," Fargo said.

"You've a convincing way of putting things," Roswall said wryly. "Take the girl and good luck."

"I'll need it," Fargo said.

The lieutenant's face grew grim. "I'm going back to take orders from a man I've no more respect for. That's going to be hard," he said.

"You won't be the first to do that in this man's army, soldier," Fargo said.

"Guess not," Roswall said. "Thanks, Fargo. You've saved all our necks. None of us will be forgetting that."

"It's likely we could be meeting again," Fargo said and strode into the serviceberry. Caryn rushed to him at once. "Get your things," he said.

"Just two bags. The general has my horse at the fort," she said.

"You'll ride with me. General Davis will have an extra mount for you," he said. Clutching her bags, Caryn climbed onto the Ovaro with a helping hand from a trooper. Roswall gave a salute as they rode away. "Till next time," Fargo called as he put the

Ovaro into a trot. Caryn rode in front of him, leaning back against him. "You underestimated him," Fargo said. She turned her head to look up at him and he saw the terrible sadness in her face.

"Yes," she said. "I didn't believe he was that ruthless."

"Some things are hard to believe," Fargo said.

"He knew I'd never reach the stage depot, didn't he?" she asked. "There was just no chance of it." He didn't answer and she turned away and rode in silence with him. He turned toward a line of bitternut when he spotted a dozen loin-clothed riders and stayed in the woods till they were out of sight. The day was drawing to an end after he avoided another band of Pawnee by halting in a cluster of black oak. Moving on, he entered another stand of bitternut as dusk descended, quickly turning into night.

"We'll bed down here," he said as he swung from the horse and helped Caryn down. She still had the dried beef strips and shared them with him as a half moon rose, filtering through the foliage as he undressed to his underwear. The night stayed warm and he watched as Caryn began to take off the blouse, not going into the trees this time. She let it hang loose but still on as she sat on her knees in front of him.

"What happens when we reach General Davis?" she asked.

"You want to know if you're going to be safe?" he asked and she nodded solemnly. "I can't say that. You've stepped into a tinderbox. There's every chance none of us will make it. There's no sense in fooling you."

"No, I wouldn't want that," she said. "If tomorrow's a question mark, then I want to enjoy now." She shrugged her shoulders and the yellow blouse fell to her waist. Rising, she pulled off the rest of her clothes and faced him beautifully naked. His eyes enjoyed gently rounded shoulders, long arms, a long, narrow waist, and breasts that stood high and forward, curbing slowly at the tops to full, firm cups. Very pale pink areolas circled each almost flat little nipple, each tiny protrusion also the palest pink. Her long, narrow waist curved into narrow hips and a flat abdomen where a very tiny indentation was hardly visible. Below it, an almost concave belly swelled slightly where it met the Venus mound covered by a modest, black, fibrous nap. Long legs, thighs, and calves were fashioned of slow curves. Her skin, tight and absolutely unblemished, glowed milk white under the moonlight.

Strangely, she gave the appearance of being thin when she was not at all thin, everything well covered on her, everything rounded and seamless. She leaned forward and her breasts pressed into his chest, wonderfully soft. As his arms went around her, she seemed terribly fragile, yet there was nothing fragile in the firmness of her body. Nor in the touch of her lips, a hot hunger to them, opening for him instantly, her tongue sliding out, touching, pushing, caressing. Her hand reached down, took his, and pressed it to one softly firm breast. He let his thumb slowly rub the almost flat pale pink tip, circle the tiny areola, and caress the tip again until he felt it grow and become a tiny protuberance.

"Aaaah . . . ah, ah, yes, yes," Caryn Cogwell whispered. "I want to forget today and ignore tomorrow. Help me." He answered by gently drawing her breast deep into his mouth, caressing the sweet fullness of it. She groaned, a low, guttural sound yet fashioned of utter pleasure. His hand slid downward and traced an invisible line along the flatness of her abdomen, then down further as he continued to suck upon her breast. The guttural cries grew louder and more breathless. He reached lower and pushed his hand into the modest nap, enjoying the soft fibrous feel of it and the soft rise of her Venus mound. "Oh God, oh, yes, yes . . . oh, oh." She gasped and he felt her long thighs fall open, close at once, open again, close. She moaned suddenly as his hand moved lower and came to rest at the end of the little V, where he could feel the dampness of her.

He pushed lower and gently invaded the tight moistness where her thighs were pressed together. With a sharp cry she let her legs fall open and he reached down, pausing as she clamped his hand in a warm, moist vise. She held it there, and he felt her trembling until with a rush of breath she let her thighs fall open again and this time her hips lifted, fell back, and lifted again in wordless entreaty. He let his hand slide forward to touch the soft, roscid lips. They quivered as he stroked again, moving deeper, and Caryn gave a shuddering sigh of delight. "Yes, yes, yes, yes," she murmured and he felt her torso rise and twist, the moist lips palpitating for him. He drew his mouth from her breast only to have her thrust it forward again even as her hands clasped his muscled thighs and pulled him atop her.

His throbbing maleness came against the pubic mound, where it rested for a moment. She half screamed at the sensation as she drew her nap upward, lifting, seeking. He let himself touch the dark, warm portal. As he slid forward, her thighs rose and clasped around him with a soft suddenness. Little cries came from her, pleadings that needed no words, demands that needed no voice. She moved upward with him, encompassing him, drawing in all of him. Her low groans filled the

77

night. He responded to her rhythm, letting her set the pace. She was deliciously slow at first, drawing out each movement, sliding up and down his warm gift, drawing every pulsating sensation she could from it. Her arms circled his neck. She kept his mouth against her breasts as her lips moved against the side of his neck in nibbling strokes that echoed the rhythm of her other lips. He felt her desert slowness, the flesh unwilling to bow to the mind, asserting its own demands, and suddenly she was surging forward, her warm, dark, sweet walls stroking him with a new urgency.

"Oh, yes, I want, I want," she murmured and she clung to him inside and outside, every part of her pressed to him, every part of her finding a place to touch, to contact, to join with. Murmured words turned into gasps and gasps turned into cries and suddenly cries turned into screams as her body began to pump furiously with him, thighs and arms clasped tightly around him, her breasts quivering under his lips. He was one with her when the final scream burst from her to hang in the air, a combination of ecstasy and despair. She stayed wrapped around him, her cries finally becoming half sobs that clung to pleasure until there was only the quivering memory of sensations ended yet never ending.

As he lay with her, she held him inside her, legs keeping him in place. "Stay," she whispered. "Stay." Finally, with a sigh of reluctance, she let him slide from her but kept his face to her breasts and he held her to him until she was suddenly asleep. He looked at the loveliness of her and realized helping her forget was a small gift. Ecstasy would be hers again. Pleasure would come and go, as would pain. But what she had learned about the man who had fathered her would never leave. To be rejected left a terrible pain. To be discarded left a terrible hate. He wondered how she would live with that and he felt sorry for her. He closed his eyes finally, and she slept clinging to him until the new day dawned.

She woke when he rose and he took the time to enjoy her long-waisted, sinuous body as she stretched in a serpentine motion and sat up to wrap her arms around him. The smooth softness of her breasts pressed against his chest as he held her. "It was wonderful," she said. "It could be habit forming."

"It could," he agreed. "If I can find the time and place."

"I've confidence in you," she said as he pulled back, rose, and dressed. Then he saddled the pinto and rode from the trees with Caryn in front of him. By midday he had made two side trips into cover to avoid fast-riding Pawnee parties. A third one took him behind a rock formation and when the riders went on he paused to peer down at an armband on the ground. His lips drew back in a grimace. The Cheyenne had arrived. Time was getting shorter. He pressed the Ovaro into a faster trot and finally reached the Smoky River. As the day neared to an end the field camp came into sight. Soon after, he was standing before Miles Davis with Caryn. He told her story first, and spared no words in the telling.

Miles Davis was too fine a gentleman and too good an officer to be anything but understanding with Caryn. "That's a shocking story, my dear. I feel for you. I've never liked your father but this paints him with a terrible brush," he said. "You're welcome here. I only wish I could offer you a place of safety but we may all be on borrowed time."

"Fargo told me," Caryn said.

"There's one bright spot," the general said and

turned to Fargo. "A month ago I sent a request to Washington for extra reinforcements. If they were going to turn it down they'd have done so by now so I expect new troops any day now. If we can just keep the lid on things, reinforcements might discourage the tribes from attacking."

"How'd you send the request? Courier?" Fargo asked.

"It had to go through Cogwell, army procedures and regulations. You know the army works on rules and regulations."

"Shit, what if he turned it down?"

"He can't. It had to go through him so's he kept aware but he can't do anything but send it on. Only Washington can turn it down or approve it," Miles said.

"Let's be grateful for that," Fargo said.

"I think this young lady could stand something to eat and a good night's rest," the general said. "I'll have the mess sergeant bring you both something. There are two tents right outside you can use."

"Thank you. I'll try not to be a burden," Caryn answered.

"You won't be. I'm just terribly sorry for the reason that brought you here," Miles said and Fargo walked from his tent with Caryn. Outside, he helped take her bags into the first of two one-person pup tents.

"I'll come visit later," she said.

"Impossible. There'll be a sentry on all night just outside," he said.

"Don't assume things. I want to talk to you about something," she said and he saw the disturbed furrow crease her brow. He nodded and left her and strode to the next tent. After the mess sergeant brought him a meal he undressed and stretched out on the cot. He was almost asleep when Caryn slipped into the tent and he sat up. She sat down on the edge of the cot, her lips on his at once.

"Thought you were going to talk," he said.

"In a minute," she said and her lips moved with his, her breasts pressing against him. Finally she drew back. "Damn. Right time, wrong place," she muttered.

He held her as she stayed against him. "Talk," he said.

The little furrow came to her brow and she looked disturbed again. "It's about what General Davis said, his request to Washington for more troops," she began. "I was snooping through my father's files in his office. He caught me but not before I'd gone through a number of papers. I think one of them was General Davis's request."

"Shit," Fargo bit out. "You're saying he never sent the request through."

She turned her hands up helplessly. "General Davis said he hasn't the authority to turn it down but if he just sits on it the results are the same."

"No reinforcements," Fargo said.

"The trouble is I'm not sure. I just skimmed over army papers. I was looking for personal things. I'm just not sure," Caryn said almost apologetically.

"We have to be sure. I've got to find out if you saw that request. A lot of lives will depend on it," Fargo said.

"You going to tell General Davis?"

"Not till I know. Can't see any good in telling him now. He can't do anything but worry more."

"He can start thinking about plans for the worst," Caryn said.

He turned her words over in his mind and decided there was a bitter logic to them. "You tell him when he comes asking in the morning. I'll be on my way by then," he said.

"What I saw was in the first drawer of the metal file cabinet," Caryn said and her lips came to his and lingered until she pulled away. The troubled frown went with her as she hurried from the tent. He lay back on the cot and gathered sleep to himself, waking only when the first streaks of dawn touched the sky. He dressed quickly and rode from the field camp with only the sentries watching. He kept a steady pace and avoided roving bands of braves, timing his journey so that dark lay over Fort Travis when he neared it. He hung back and rested himself and the Ovaro in a cluster of hackberry as the settlements on the edge of the fort closed in for the night. He continued to wait, watching the fort as it grew still, the horses stabled, the troopers barracked. Cogwell had only three sentries outside the walls of the fort. He plainly did not expect Indian trouble.

He seemed confident that trouble would aim at Miles in the northern plains. Perhaps too confident. Fargo frowned and the thought clung, unsettling. He put it aside as his eyes swept the fort. After letting another hour pass, he tethered the Ovaro to a low branch. He took the lariat with him as he moved on foot in a half crouch and made his way to the rear corner of the stockade walls. A quick check of the sentries showed that they stayed patrolling at the front of the fort. Fargo tossed the lariat in the air. On the third try, the loop caught the top of the stockade posts and he pulled it tight. Testing it first, he began to pull himself up the side of the stockade until he reached the top of the posts. Holding on with one hand, he tossed the remainder of the lariat over the other side. When it hit the ground, he began to lower himself until he touched down inside the stockade.

Leaving the lariat in place against the posts, he set off in a crouch again, moving through the silence inside the fort. Passing the low row of stables, he paused as he saw half the stable doors were open, the stalls inside without horses. It meant only one thing. A good part of the force was not in the fort and the frown stayed with him as he went on to the commander's quarters. Cogell's office was at the left, he remembered, and he carefully pressed the door until it opened. Pausing, he let the faint light from the lamps near the stable creep into the room. Straining his eyes, he found the wood desk and the kerosene lamp atop it. Closing the door behind him, he groped his way across the room until he reached the desk. He used a lucifer in his pocket to turn the lamp on low. The tentative yellow light spread out and the file cabinet took shape behind the desk. He went to it at once, pulled the top drawer open, and took out the thick file folder.

He laid it on the desk, opened it, and began to rifle through the papers inside it. He had gone through almost a quarter of the stack when he halted, his eyes fastening on the communiqué in front of him:

> To: The Department of the Army
>   Washington, D.C.
>   From: Brigadier General Miles Davis,
>   Commander, 3rd Army Corps,
>   Department of the Missouri
> Request for immediate reinforcements,
> minimum 100 cavalry troops. Situation
> very unstable. Please dispatch at once.

Miles' signature followed the request and Fargo's curse stayed silent inside him. Caryn hadn't been mistaken. The request languished in the file folder, a plea that would never be answered, a death warrant *in absentia*. He was staring at it, letting his bitter thoughts consume his being, always a mistake, he knew as the voice broke the silence. "Keep your hands in the air," it said. Fargo froze, instantly recognizing the icy superiority of it. He kept his hand motionless as he looked up. Cogwell stood by the door, a Colt New Model army pistol in his hands, a good single-action, six-shot weapon, accurate and fast. "Take your gun out, very slowly," Cogwell ordered.

Fargo used two fingers to lift his Colt from its holster and let it drop to the floor. "You've good ears," he commented.

"I was awake, saw the light from under the door," the general said. "Move back, hands up." Fargo swore silently. The revolver was pointed steadily at him. There was no way it could miss. Cogwell stepped forward, scooped the Colt from the floor, and took the document from the file folder. "Should have gotten rid of this when it came. What made you come looking?" he questioned.

Fargo chose his words carefully. So far as Cogwell knew, Caryn was dead. He wanted to be sure and keep it that way. "Miles told me about the request. But the troops haven't arrived. I figured to find out why," he said. "I got my answer."

Cogwell seemed to accept the explanation. "And now you're going to get a firing squad." He motioned with the pistol. "Outside, walk real slow in front of me." Fargo stepped from the office with Cogwell following. "Sentries," the general shouted and the three sentries came on the run. "How'd this man get past you?" Cogwell barked angrily.

"We didn't see him, sir," one of the sentries said, embarrassment flooding his face.

"None of us did," another added.

"This'll be on your records," Cogwell snapped. "Put him in the guardhouse, two guards outside at all times. Think you can do that?"

"Yes, sir," the three soldiers answered as one.

"Then send Lieutenant Roswall to me," Cogwell said as the three sentries surrounded Fargo and began to march him down the length of the fort. When they reached the end of the stables, Fargo saw the small, square guardhouse standing off by itself. The door was opened and he was pushed into the structure, a lamp burning in one corner. Fargo saw the single room was divided into two cells, a cot in each. Both barred doors hung open and his guards left them that way as they slammed the front door after him. Fargo swept the guardhouse with his eyes. There was a single barred window at one side and stone walls that rose from a stone floor to a stone roof. There'd be no cutting, digging, or sawing one's way out of the house, he saw. The throwing knife was still in his calf holster but he realized there'd be a damn slim chance of using it.

Yet he'd wait and hope. He'd no other choice, he reminded himself as he lowered himself onto the cot in the nearest of the divided rooms. He stretched out and let himself catnap until morning finally came to wander in through the lone barred window. When the door to the guardhouse opened, three soldiers entered, two holding carbines pointed at him, the third with morning rations of bread and water. Wordlessly they left the rations and the door closed after them. Fargo ate the bread and drank the water, suddenly aware of the emptiness of his stomach. When he finished, he examined each corner of the guardhouse, hoping to discover some flaw, a chink missing, anything that might offer a chance for escape.

But there was nothing. He'd have to have the throwing knife ready the next time he had visitors. It seemed his only chance. He guessed it was noon when the door clicked open. Fargo drew the thin blade from its calf holster and pushed it up the sleeve of his shirt. He was standing when the door opened and he was surprised to see the youthful, blond-haired face of Lieutenant Roswall step into the guardhouse, revolver in hand. Two soldiers with carbines followed him, halting when he did. "Wait outside. I'll be all right," he said to the two troopers, who backed from the house and shut the door. Roswall lowered his gun and his voice. "Jesus, Fargo, what the hell were you doing?" he asked.

"Had to find out something," Fargo said. "Where's Cogwell?"

"In his office, filling out all the correct forms to execute a thief. He wants to be sure everything's done right. I've orders to choose a firing squad for dawn tomorrow," Roswall said.

"I'm not going to just wait around," Fargo said and let the throwing knife come down into his hand. "I'll use it," he said.

Roswall eyed the blade. "It won't work. They won't back off because you've a hostage. They'll shoot," he said. "But there's a way."

"I'm listening," Fargo said.

"I know I'm alive because of you. The six troopers that were with me feel the same. We owe you and we'll get you out of here," the lieutenant said.

"How?"

"One of them will look in on you at midnight. You'll take him hostage with this," Roswall said and drew a Darling six-barreled pepperbox from his pocket and handed it to him. "We'll tell the general you had it in your boot."

Fargo took the little derringerlike pistol with its short, automatically rotating barrels. "But you said they'd shoot, hostage or not," he reminded Roswall.

"That's right, only the sentries are going to be the troopers that were with me. They'll hold back and play their parts. You'll make it out of the fort. Your horse is where you left him," the lieutenant said.

"My Colt?"

"The general gave it to the equipment sergeant. One of my men will have it for you," Roswall said.

Fargo put the knife away and extended his hand. "I'm obliged, Lieutenant, real obliged."

"One good turn deserves another," Roswall said, clasping Fargo's hand.

"The general's going to be real mad at your men," Fargo said.

"We have our stories down. All he can do is accuse us of poor judgment," Roswall said.

"Why is half the stable empty?" Fargo questioned.

"The general sent a special escort to bring Howard Elliman here from Independence," Roswall said.

"Who's Howard Elliman?"

"Secretary of the Army. The general invited him to visit the fort. They'll be here in another day or two," Roswall said.

"But Cogwell knows the north plains are close to exploding," Fargo said.

"He's confident the secretary will be safe here in Fort Travis." Roswall said and turned to leave. "Midnight. Be ready," the lieutenant said and left. Fargo lowered himself onto the cot, the frown digging deeper into his brow. Cogwell hadn't invited the secretary of the army just to show off Fort Travis. The pieces were beginning to fit. Cogwell's confidence was taking on new meaning. His ambition matched his ruthlessness. He not only expected the Indian uprising in the north plains to wipe out Miles and his command and the settlers, he had planned for it to happen.

But there'd be a few survivors that would make it to the fort. Cogwell wanted Howard Elliman there to hear their stories himself. It'd be a searing experience. More pieces were falling into place as Fargo frowned at the enormity of Cogwell's planning. And his cleverness. He'd made use of the forces that were already smoldering in place to serve his own ambition. He'd planned and timed every part of it. Caryn had been an unexpected intrusion. It was no wonder he had to get rid of her so quickly. She might have been more of a problem than she had intended to be. Fargo swore silently. Was it too late, he wondered. Were the forces Cogwell had set in motion beyond stopping, now inexorably moving with a power of their own. Was there still a moment, a fragile possibility? He thought of Little Bird as he knew he had to somehow try to halt the march of death.

He lay back on the cot and cursed at how slowly time sometimes moved. Night came to the lone barred window, then the faint light of the moon, and finally he heard the click of the door. He rose, the little pepperbox pistol in hand as the trooper stepped quickly across the room to Fargo. "Go through the motions, just in case somebody should be watching," the trooper said. Fargo nodded and pressed the little pistol into the back of the soldier's neck as he marched the man out of the guardhouse. Outside, a sentry raised his rifle and Fargo paused but saw the man's quick nod and hurried on with his hostage. He crossed the dark courtyard with the gun jammed against the man and reached the stockade doors, where two more sentries appeared, their rifles raised.

But they backed off even as they seemed to want to shoot. The trooper he held as hostage stayed against him as Fargo left the stockade. "Stay back, Jesus," the man called to the two sentries as he drew Fargo's Colt from his pocket and pressed it into his hand. Fargo dropped the little pepperbox as he took the Colt, pushing the trooper with him another dozen yards. "Thank the others for me," he whispered as he pushed the soldier to the ground and broke into a run. He cut behind the first line of tents beyond the fort and ran between others, quickly reaching the hackberry and the Ovaro. Climbing onto the horse, he rode into the night until he found a place to bed down until morning. When dawn came he found a rare patch of good bluegrass and let the horse feed. When the Ovaro finished, Fargo rode north at a fast pace. He was riding hard, in a hurry to get to Miles, thinking too hard about what lay ahead.

He'd let his usual caution desert him and he realized it as the arrow grazed the side of his head as he passed a line of black oak. In an instinctive, instant reaction, he swerved the pinto right, into the trees, and cursed in pain as the low branch slammed into his forehead. He felt himself falling backward from the horse and flashing lights exploded inside his head. They became a gray curtain as he hit the ground. He lay there, shaking his head. He felt the pain, but the gray curtain lifted. He looked up at the six figures that stared down at him, each with the heavy-featured faces of the Pawnee. They reached down and yanked him to his feet. When he grabbed for the Colt, he found only an empty holster; then he saw the gun in the hands of one of the Pawnee.

The Indians gestured to the Ovaro as they climbed onto their mounts. Fargo pulled himself onto the pinto and the Pawnee closed around him at once. They kept him in a tight circle as they moved forward with him. They could have riddled him with arrows and he wondered why they hadn't as they rode north with him.

6

As they rode across the open land, Fargo spotted a distant lone lookout on his short-legged Indian pony. He found another to the south on a high mound. Then, as the Pawnee rode north further with him, he saw a third lookout to the west. He felt his heart sink. They had posted lookouts across the prairie. Events were rolling to a terrible climax. Another quarter mile on his captors slowed and Fargo saw the lone rider come down from a ridge to meet them. As the figure drew closer he recognized the courier that had met with Bart Whitman. The Pawnee halted, Fargo inside their circle, and the courier spoke to them in short sentences, then turned to Fargo.

"You ride alone to the river where the soldiers camp. Why?" he asked.

"Just going that way," Fargo said.

"You bring message," the Pawnee said.

"No," Fargo answered and had the reason they hadn't simply killed him. They suspected him of being a courier. "No message," he repeated. The Pawnee turned to the others and barked commands that Fargo managed to understand.

"Take him to Tall Tree," the Indian said and the others moved off with Fargo at once. Fargo rode quietly as his thoughts raced. He wanted to confront the Pawnee chief and try to reach him, but not in his camp, not with the

Cheyenne, Kiowa, Kansa, and Osage looking on. The Pawnee chief was intransigent enough. Outsiders would only stiffen his own attitudes. But Fargo realized he'd only one option left and his glance went to the six riders that encircled him. He'd have to find a moment, a split second that would give him a chance to escape. The moment came an hour later when the Pawnee turned into the forest of bur oaks that eventually led to the main camp. The thickness of the forest didn't allow them to surround him as they rode. Four of the Indians rode in front of him and two beside him, one on each side of him.

Fargo waited and he saw that the Pawnee on his left had the Colt tucked into the band of his loincloth. They had all relaxed some, sure of their captive, and Fargo murmured silent thanks for the dubious rewards of complacency. He let his hand steal down to the calf holster around his leg, keeping one eye on the Indian beside him. The man rode with his body relaxed, his eyes on his companions riding ahead. Fargo drew the double-edged blade slowly, but when it cleared its sheath he struck with the speed and silence of a diamondback. His arm came up in a slashing blow that almost took the Pawnee's head off. The Indian hadn't yet toppled from his horse when Fargo twisted in the saddle and swiped a flat arc at the rider on his left.

The Indian had started to turn when the blow struck. His mouth fell open soundlessly and Fargo yanked the Colt from his loincloth belt before he began to fall from his horse in a slow, sideways motion. Transferring the Colt to his right hand, Fargo saw the two Indians in front of him turn to look back as they heard the first rider hit the ground. The Colt barked twice and both the figures jerked convulsively on their ponies before they dropped to the forest floor. The last two Pawnee had sent their mounts into the trees in a tight circle to come back at him from opposite sides. Fargo ducked an arrow that grazed his hat and ducked again as another smashed into a tree just beside him. He was too good a target on the Ovaro with no room to maneuver, he realized. As he leaped sideways from the horse, another arrow narrowly missed him.

He hit the ground on the balls of his feet. Going into a low crouch, he saw a thick stand of five-foot horseweed. He dived into the coarse leaves and fell to one knee. He heard the remaining two Pawnee drop to the ground to avoid being targets themselves. Listening, he heard them move toward the horseweed. But they moved tentatively, slowly. They didn't know where he was hiding. Again, using his ears as eyes, he heard them separate and start forward on both sides of the horseweed. He stayed low, the Colt raised in his hand, his eyes peering through the weeds and dry forest brush. He cursed silently. In true Indian fashion, they were moving noiselessly on the balls of moccasined feet, easily his match in stealthiness.

He stayed motionless, hidden in the thickness of the horseweeds. They hadn't yet seen him, he was confident, yet he knew how little that meant with the Indian. His Colt had been fired. It smelled of gunpowder. They'd pick up the scent, as they would the odor of leather and wool. His lips pulled back in a grimace. They still hadn't seen him but by now they damn well knew where he was. He could only wait as his eyes flicked from side to side, searching for the movement of a leaf, the sway of a stem. Suddenly he saw it, a stem shuddering, then another following. He half turned, aimed the Colt, and peered into the brush. But the explosion of sound came from behind him, leaves being trampled, a short, hissing roar of triumph.

He spun and saw the figure leaping at him with tomahawk raised. He fired the Colt. His first shot missed, but he managed to correct his aim as the Indian flew through the air at him. His second shot struck home at almost point-blank range, and the Pawnee's chest exploded in a shower of red. Fargo rolled to the side as the man's body landed facedown where he had been crouched. Starting to turn himself around, Fargo had time only to see the second figure diving at him, tomahawk in hand. He tried to duck away but the short-handled ax came down against the side of his arm. As he cursed in pain he felt the Colt fall from his hand and he just managed to avoid another short blow of the tomahawk. Bringing an arm up, he jammed it into the Pawnee's throat as the Indian came at him again. The man gagged, fell back, and his blow went wide. Fargo lifted a short uppercut that caught the Indian's chin flush enough to send his head back. Bringing a left around in a flat arc, Fargo crashed his fist into the man's jaw and the figure fell sideways.

The Pawnee started to get up, the tomahawk still in his hand, when Fargo's kick caught him in the solar plexus. Gasping for breath, the Indian fell back for a moment, long enough for Fargo to grab the tomahawk and twist it from his grasp. With a guttural roar, the Pawnee dived at him, a tackling dive that sent him falling backward. A flash of metal caught Fargo's eye and he saw a hunting knife in the Indian's hand. Out of position for a proper blow, Fargo could only bring the tomahawk up in a flat, sideways blow that slammed into his assailant's shoulder. It was enough to make the man's knife thrust miss as it plunged down and it gave Fargo room to bring the tomahawk down in a short, chopping blow. It landed against the side of the Indian's head and the man pitched forward. He drew himself up and turned. Blood streaming from the side of his face, the Pawnee lunged forward with the hunting knife. Fargo had time only to throw the tomahawk in a short, overhand toss as the Indian flew at him. But it was enough as the blade slammed into the forehead of the lunging figure and hung there for a moment before falling away.

Fargo scooted back on his haunches as the Pawnee pitched forward, his forehead all but split in two. Pushing to his feet, Fargo saw the figure shudder for a long moment and then lie still. His arm throbbing from where the tomahawk had struck, Fargo retrieved his Colt and slowly walked to where the Ovaro had halted. He waited a long moment to regain his breath and accommodate himself to the throbbing of his arm before he pulled himself onto the horse. Slowly, he nosed the pinto out of the stand of bur oak. Sweeping the flatland before him, he rode east.

It was near dusk when he reached the Smoky Hill fork and dark when he arrived at the field camp. A soldier helped him down from the Ovaro and he saw Caryn running toward him from a tent. "Oh God, we were so worried when you didn't come back," she said.

"You had reason," he said. "There's a small bottle in my saddlebag with a staghorn stopper." She reached into the saddlebag and came out with the bottle as Miles appeared. "Rub this on my arm while we talk," he said. "White willow bark compress with briony and balm of Gilead. Great for bruises." He went into the office with Miles and sat across from him as Caryn rubbed the ointment into his arm. "Caryn was right," Fargo said. "He never sent the request through."

"There won't be any reinforcements," the general said gravely.

Fargo nodded and recounted everything that had happened. "It all fits," he said when he finished. "Including the six fake troopers that attacked the chief's daughter. Bart Whitman didn't send them. Cogwell did. That explains their uniforms. Whitman was selling guns to the Pawnee. He didn't have to stir them up to do it. Cogwell was doing it for him."

"Why?" Caryn put in.

"The general touched on it when we first talked. Your father wanted command of the entire territory. When the brass didn't go for that he decided to show them that Miles couldn't handle his command," Fargo said.

"Yes, it becomes clear now," Miles Davis said, more sadness than anger in his voice. "First, under the guise of troop rotation he gave me new, inexperienced men with no training in fighting the Indians. Second, he began to find ways to stir up the Pawnee, to inflame an already explosive climate. Then he shelved my request for reinforcements."

"It's one way to make a name for yourself. You set the house on fire, fix it so the fire chief can't put out the fire, and show how incompetent he was. You win, everybody else loses," Fargo said.

"He's willing to have hundreds of people slaughtered to further his ambitions," Miles said, awe in his voice.

"Hard to believe about a fellow officer and gentleman?" Fargo said. "Ask Caryn. She's learned all about what's hard to believe."

The general's eyes held on Caryn. "I can't pretend to know what you must feel, my dear," he said.

Caryn's lips thinned. "Hate. That's what I feel, General, hate," she bit out. She rose, walked to the tent flap, and stared out into the night, arms folded across her breasts. Fargo spoke to Miles.

"What do you figure to do now?" he asked.

"I don't know. There's not a lot of choices," he said.

"I'm going to try to reach Tall Tree. I'll use Little Bird to get to him. Maybe I can reason with him."

Miles returned a weary smile. "You can't reason with

96

a burning flame. But try, for God's sake try," he said. He was still sitting in his chair as Fargo walked from the tent with Caryn.

"This Pawnee girl, how are you going to get her to co-operate?" Caryn asked outside in front of the pup tent.

Fargo paused a moment and decided there was no time left for games. "I'll do whatever I have to," he said.

"Whatever you have to," Caryn repeated. "That's taking in a lot."

"There's a helluva lot at stake," Fargo said.

Caryn thought for a moment. "Yes," she murmured finally. "You do whatever you have to. I'm going to hope it's just asking." She turned and left him. He went into the tent, pulled off his clothes, and lay down on the cot as exhaustion swept over his body. He slept heavily and didn't wake till the sun warmed the tent. He opened his eyes to see Caryn seated at the edge of the cot. She had the yellow blouse on, but open down the front, her breasts thrusting forward for him to see. He took in their loveliness, the small, flat tips and pale pink areolas.

"So you'll remember," she said.

"Didn't need reminding," he said.

"Good," she said, pulling the blouse closed. Then, buttoning it, she hurried from the tent. He rose, washed, and dressed and was grateful that the troopers had fed and rubbed down his horse. He rode from the camp, his arm still throbbing but with far less pain. Riding with caution this time, he made his way west, avoiding lone lookouts astride their ponies and racing bands of braves until he finally reached the round rock and the quiet arbor behind it with the carpet of cerise-lavender blazing stars. He dismounted, walked forward in the late-afternoon sun, and when he saw the movement beside a cedar, he halted, one hand on the Colt immediately. But the figure that stepped into the open moved with sinuous grace, her long, jet black hair trailing down her back.

"I wondered if you were coming back," she said.

"I did not mean to be so long," he said. "Do you remember what I asked you to do?"

She gave a wry little smile. "You asked me to remember your lips."

"And to talk to Tall Tree."

"The first was easy. The second impossible. He will not listen to me."

"Maybe he will listen to me," Fargo said. "I want you to bring him here, let me talk to him."

She frowned back and he wondered if he caught a moment of fear cross her face. "If I do that, we can never meet again. He will see to that," she said. "Is that what you want?"

"No, it is what I must do, for your people, too," he told her.

"It is not what your lips told me to remember. It is not what I want to give to you," she said and in her smoldering, liquid, black eyes he saw resentment. "But after what you have done for me, I must give something back to you. It is our way, I told you."

"Must you give only one thing?" he asked.

She peered back, thoughts tumbling through her. "It is that way, our way," she said after a moment.

"Old ways can change," he slid at her.

A tiny smile came to her lips, something made of slyness and discovery. "Yes. It has happened before. We will make it happen again," she said, and whipping the thin rawhide belt from her waist, she shook her shoulders and the elkskin dress fell from her and she stood beautifully, proudly naked before him. He heard his breath draw in at the beauty of her, slender yet shapely, her skin an ochre-tinged hue that glowed in the sunlight, her breasts high and beautifully formed, nipples a light brown that stood erect, inviting, each circled by a pale brown areola. A flat stomach and slightly curved abdomen were followed by a small, almost childish nap. She held her thighs slightly apart as her hips thrust forward. She combined a regality with a sensuousness that radiated from inside her.

He reached his arms out and she came to him, all soft, smooth warmness, and he smelled the faint sweet, musky scent of oakmoss. Her fingers helped him unbutton his shirt, and in moments he lay with her on the soft flowers and his hand curled around one high breast. He caressed it and brought his lips down to the pale brown nipples. A little sigh came from her and he saw her lips half open in pleasure. He sucked and gently pulled on the firm mounds and heard her sighs grow longer. He brought his hand down across her ochre skin, the smooth, satiny feel of her, and pressed slowly downward to the tiny nap and felt its softness, a surprising and exciting sensation. Her pubic mound was small and very smooth under the softness of her hair, and her legs rose and opened up for him. He slid his hand down further and explored the warm portal she had opened for him. Her hips rose and twisted from side to side, and then fell back, thrusting upward again.

Her body began to move with a slow, sinuous motion and he listened for sounds of pleasure, soft groans, or escalating cries. But there was nothing except her long sighs and he lifted his head to look at her. Her eyes were closed, her mouth open, lips drawn back in a smile of pleasure, but there were no sounds save the long sighs. He half turned and brought his warm, throbbing organ over her silken nap. She trembled as she lifted her hips and thrust herself upward for him. Her long sighs grew longer but no louder and as he brought himself slowly to her, he felt the smooth thighs close against him. She caught his hand and brought it to her high breasts, which were gently bouncing as she thrust herself upward. Her neck arched backward and her lips were open and he waited for a cry to burst from her. But there was none and her warm tunnel rose up and pushed itself around him. He pressed forward, deep, and felt the tightness of her around him.

She began to slide back and forth with him, each motion a sinuous, pleasure-filled act, and her sighs were a seemingly endless, sibilant sound. She held his hand to her breasts as she writhed with him and he felt the fervor of her growing wilder. She pumped against him, quick, frantic motions now, and her sighs were short, staccato hisses, urgent and ecstatic, yet still no more than sighs. Suddenly he felt her stiffen, her warm, moist walls vibrating furiously around him. He saw her eyes come open and stare at him, a wild disbelief in the liquid orbs. Her mouth reached for his as she pulled him to her, clinging against him, her body shaking wildly. Her eyes stayed wide, staring, as if she watched from someplace outside her body until finally, her head arching backward, she held herself stiffly against him. Suddenly even the sighs were gone and there was only a soundless cry of ecstasy, her mouth open in a wordless, silent smile. Only when her body relaxed in a sudden almost collapsing motion did another long sigh shudder through her. She held his face to her breasts and cradled his head against her until she fell back and stared up at him.

He looked at the beauty of her, at the small, dreamy smile that came to her lips. "It was good," he said. "Very good."

"Yes," she whispered. "Good, very good."

He pushed away a strand of the long jet hair. "I never knew ecstasy could be silent," he said, as much to himself as to her. She frowned back, not understanding. "You never cried out," he said. "You didn't hold back yet you never cried out."

Her smile grew wistful. "We are raised not to show pain or pleasure," she said. "Especially the daughter of a chief. We are raised to keep things within us."

"Sometimes it is better to let go," he said. "It brings more pleasure."

"More?" she asked with a frown.

"More." He laughed and enjoyed her lips again.

"I would like to cry out for you," she said with sudden seriousness. "If there could be another time."

"Maybe there will be," he said.

"No," she said and sat up, her high breasts hardly moving as she reached to put on the elkskin dress.

Was fatalism part of her background? Or a wisdom beyond his? He refused to accept either. "Never say no," he told her and stood up as she rose.

"I must go now," she said. "I will come again in the morning."

"With your father," he said.

She nodded, unsmiling. "It is what you want," she said.

"I want you to want it, too," he called after her as she walked from him.

"I cannot," she said, pausing to look back. "But you have let me give what I wanted to give you. It must be enough." She hurried on and he lowered himself to the soft carpet of flowers. The sun was gone now and the shadows were sliding over the land. The dark came quickly and he stretched out on his bedroll and let himself sleep, awaking with the first streaks of dawn. He rose, dressed, and led the Ovaro into the surrounding trees, where the horse wouldn't be seen from the leafy alcove.

He waited and let himself nibble on a length of dried beef strip, drank from his canteen, and stepped into the border of trees as the sun flooded the scene. Little Bird appeared first and then, a half-dozen paces behind her, the tall, austere figure of the Pawnee chief in his beaded vest and leggings. The girl halted, waiting, and Fargo stepped from the trees. He saw the chief's eyes widen in surprise, then turn to Little Bird with anger. She spoke quickly, explaining, saying things his knowledge of Caddoan didn't let him understand. But he needed no language to understand the harshness of the Pawnee chief's face as he turned and glared at him. Fargo met his angry gaze and spoke to Little Bird without looking at her.

"Tell him I know he is a great chief," Fargo began and hoped even a Pawnee chief wasn't immune to flattery. "Only a great chief would hear what I have to say," he went on as Little Bird translated.

"Talk," the chief cut in curtly.

Fargo drew a deep breath as he began. "I read signs. I have seen them everywhere. The Pawnee will lead other tribes to make war. If you do, the land will fill with soldiers. There will be killing and more killing. This cannot be, not for my people and not for yours. Do not do this. Do not make war," he said.

He saw only contempt in the Indian's eyes when Little Bird finished, an icy disdain forming in his face. "You come begging to the Pawnee," he said.

"Not begging. Asking," Fargo said. "For what is best for all."

"Begging," the chief snapped sharply. "Because you know you will all die. We will take back our land. I, chief of the Pawnee, will lead all the others. Nothing can change that. The Great Spirit has spoken."

"There will be only killing, no winning," Fargo said.

"We will win and you will die. You know this and you

are afraid," the chief said and Fargo swore silently at words that held too much truth. "I, Tall Tree, will be the chief of all chiefs. The winds shall speak my name forever. The Great Spirit has chosen me. It must be. It will be," he thundered. Then he turned and shot rapid-fire words at his daughter and whirled and strode away. Fargo waited until he disappeared into the trees and saw Little Bird turn and start to follow him.

"What did he say to you?" Fargo asked.

"He said that I am no longer the daughter of a chief," she answered quietly.

"Don't go. Come with me," Fargo said and knew it was an impulsive statement. "I'll find a place for you."

"I have a place. With the other women in the camp," she said. She smiled, a sweet-sad smile. "Some nice things are not to be," she said and hurried on. He didn't call after her again. He had nothing to add. Angry and frustrated, he strode into the trees, untied the Ovaro, and rode from the meeting place. In open land, he skirted Indian lookouts once more. He took a circuitous route but finally reached the river and before the day was out, the field camp.

Caryn was with Miles when he strode into the command tent. "You struck out," she said at once.

"You've become a mind reader?" he said crossly as he flung himself into a chair.

"It's in your face," she said.

He turned his eyes to Miles. "Goddamn waste of time. He wouldn't listen," Fargo said bitterly. "Thought about it all the way back here. They're different yet the same."

"Who?" the general asked.

"Cogwell and the Pawnee," Fargo said. "Two men willing to send God knows how many people to their deaths to satisfy themselves. One is a maniac driven by ambition, the other a zealot driven by hate. Neither gives a damn about anything or anyone but themselves, including their daughters. One tried to have his killed. The other disowned his."

"Maniacs with obsessions," Miles said. "Different obsessions, same end."

"What do you figure to do, Miles?" Fargo questioned.

"If I had experienced troops I'd make a cavalry fight out of it. I might stand a chance. But I've only kids with no training, not in fighting the Indian," the general said. "There's nothing I can do but wait and get ready to make a stand."

"Get ready to die, you mean," Fargo said, and Miles gave a helpless shrug. "They'll hit you first, you know, from both sides of the river. They'll wipe you out. You can't stay here."

"You saying run?"

"Yes, dammit. Head for Fort Travis. If you've a day's start you might make it."

The general stared back. "Leave my post, my command? Cogwell will add dereliction of duty. I'm here to protect the settlers."

"You can't protect them if you're wiped out," Fargo said.

"We're soldiers, Fargo. Dying is part of soldiering. The army expects us to do our best, regardless of what that means," Miles said.

"Stop talking like a general. This is different. You've been set up," Fargo countered.

"I still can't run. I'm thinking of bringing every settler down here, men, women, children. We'll all make a stand together," Miles said.

"You'll all die together, dammit," Fargo threw back. "They're better off in their houses. Some might survive."

The general's lips pursed. "Maybe. I'll think some

more on that," he reflected. "Look, old friend, you've done everything you can do. You're not paid to die in this man's army. Take Caryn and go, get away. You'll get through if anyone can."

Fargo rose, the frustration and bitterness seething inside him. "I don't mind running. I don't like leaving dead heroes behind," he said and strode from the tent, paused outside, and swore into the night. He turned when he heard Caryn coming up behind him. She linked her arm in his.

"Whatever you decide," she said. "Daddy put me on borrowed time."

"Damn Miles. He can't stop thinking army," Fargo bit out.

"It's part of him, ingrained. You don't just change a lifetime of thinking, of attitudes, of codes burned inside you," Caryn said.

"That's true enough," he agreed. "The army makes a man set in his ways. It doesn't encourage imagination."

"The way you think," she said.

"I've done some thinking on it. I'll do some looking tomorrow. I just hope we're not out of time," he said.

"How will you know when we are? When it's too late to help?" Caryn asked.

"There'll be signs. There always are. You just have to read them right," he said.

"I'll come ride with you. I can't just sit by waiting," she said.

"All right," he agreed. "An hour past dawn." She brushed his cheek with her lips as she passed him and strode to the next tent. He went into the other tent and pulled off his clothes and lay down on the cot. It was all coming down to that terrible conclusion, carnage and killing waiting to erupt. There'd be no turning off the inexorable forces that had been set in motion. The best he could hope for was to find a way to limit the disaster, to deny the Indian their total victory and Cogwell his ruthless ambition.

Even that limited goal was perhaps beyond reaching. But he had to try. Besides, there was really nothing left but to try. Not selflessness. Self-preservation, the best motivator in the world.

7

Caryn was ready and waiting astride a nice army mount when he brought the Ovaro from the stable. She didn't try to make small talk and he thanked her silently for that as she rode beside him along the edge of the river. He rode east until he was directly below the Smoky Hills, then made a sharp turn north, crossed the Saline, and rode on into the hills. He paused often when they were in the center of the Smoky Hill country, as he went past the stark buttes of sandstone and into the hills beyond. His eyes traveled carefully across each hill, and moved forward to explore further. He sent the horse up one tree-covered hill after another, investigating each and every slope and ravine, and when he halted the sun was almost in the noon sky.

"You find whatever you came here to find?" Caryn asked.

"Yes. Let's get back," he said.

"Would you like to tell me?" she questioned, falling in beside him as he put the Ovaro into a steady trot.

"When we get back to the field camp. No sense in repeating everything. Besides, I've a few things to work out yet," he told her. She rode in silence with him as he reached the river. He followed it west back to the camp. The sun was still in the midafternoon sky when they rode into the camp and he had all the pieces set firmly in his mind. Lieutenant Horgan was beside Miles when Fargo strode into the command tent with Caryn. He saw the deep lines of despair, almost defeat and resignation, in the general's face.

"Have you come up with anything, old friend?" Miles asked. "I sure as hell haven't."

"I've a plan. With a little luck and a lot of discipline it can work," Fargo said. "First we bring the settlers down here, every last family."

"Decided to go along with me on that, have you?" the general said.

"With a difference. We'll bring them down in the dead of night when the Pawnee won't see us. When they get here, they and every one of your men will go into the Smoky Hills," Fargo said.

"What the hell for?" Miles frowned.

"To hide, every last one of you. There are plenty of caves, high rocks, caverns, draws, ravines, and plenty of tree cover. When the Pawnee attack your field camp they'll find nobody to kill. They'll be frustrated and furious."

"You think they'll just give up and go home?" Miles asked. "You're making a mistake if you do."

"No, they'll be in a rage. First they'll go chasing all over looking for you. They'll figure you're running south and they can catch up to you. When that doesn't happen they'll be so goddamn mad they'll head for Fort Travis."

"Who'll be caught completely by surprise. I don't like that," Miles said.

"I don't, either, but they've a good force of men there and a fort. They're in the best position to make a good fight," Fargo said. "And we'll be coming to their rescue. I expect we can be there twelve hours after they attack the fort, maybe less."

"It's a plan and it's too bad it can't work. Seems you've forgotten a few things. Even the Smoky Hills can't hide all our horses, men, and equipment. Then the Pawnee will sure pick up our tracks. It'll lead them right to us. They'll know we're in there hiding."

"Leave that to me," Fargo said. "I've just given you the broad outline. There's a lot more but time's wasting. I want to get to the settlers. They've got to be told what to expect."

Miles thought for a long moment. "I don't have anything better. It's your show, Fargo."

"Then I'll be riding to visit every settler and tell them what and when," Fargo said.

"Let me go with you. I can talk to the women. They'll have to be convinced, too," Caryn said and Fargo shrugged his agreement.

"Take Lieutenant Horgan and a platoon with you. I imagine the Pawnee will have a scout watching the settlers' cabins. You two visiting all by yourselves might make them suspicious. This way it'll look like another of our routine patrols," the general said.

"Good enough. Let's move," Fargo said and strode outside to peer at the sun. There was enough day left to reach all the settlers before sundown. Horgan had his platoon ready in double-time and they rode out with Fargo and Caryn beside them. His eyes swept the distant terrain, picking out the lone lookouts at their isolated posts. Caryn followed his eyes and managed to find at least two of the figures.

"They could send a force to attack us," she said. "Why don't they?"

"They probably would at another time. Right now they don't want to waste men. They're saving their strength for when they hit the warpath. They've learned that attacking a full cavalry platoon means casualties.

They don't know these men aren't the usual experienced cavalry troopers," Fargo answered. "Thank God," he added as the lieutenant sent the platoon up a rise in the plain that leveled out again higher up to form a high plain. The first of the settlers' cabins came into sight an hour later and the man and woman came out as the platoon halted and Fargo and Caryn dismounted. A boy and girl looked out from the cabin doorway.

"This is an unexpected visit, Lieutenant," the man said.

"You won't like it," Horgan said. "This is Skye Fargo. He's on a special assignment from General Davis."

"Tom Eberman, my wife, Clara," the man said. He was a sturdy figure with a square, weather-tanned face.

"You've got to clear out, you and all the other families," Fargo said and told them of the imminent attack that would sweep the plains.

"Leave our homes, everything we've built up, so those savages can burn it all down?" Tom Eberman said.

"It's that or have them burn it down with you in it," Fargo said, more harshly than he'd intended. "Not much of a choice, I realize. But this won't be a passing raid. This is going to be a full-scale uprising."

Caryn focused her eyes on the woman. "You've your children to think about. Stay and they'll never grow up," she said.

"Stay and it's suicide. There's no bravery in that," Fargo said to Eberman and saw the woman squeeze his arm.

"Guess not," Eberman said. "Guess you wouldn't be here asking if there was another way. What can we take with us?"

"Some clothes and your weapons. Wagons only if you have to. Be ready by midnight tomorrow. We'll be bringing everyone down together," Fargo said and moved on, the column following.

"You obviously expect another day's cushion," Caryn said as they rode. "What'd you see that made you decide that?"

"You ask too many questions," he said.

"That's how I learn things. Besides, I'm just naturally nosy," she said. "What'd you see?"

"Persistent, too," he said. "Lookouts. They're still watching."

"Meaning?"

"They'll pull in the lookouts when they've picked a time to strike. They won't need to watch anything more then," Fargo said as the second settler's dwelling came into sight, a larger house with a larger family, a man, his wife, and three almost teenage children. Fargo repeated his message, received the same initial protest, and finally the same consent. It was a pattern that repeated itself at every house, cabin, and farm until they visited the last settlement in the darkness. As they rode back in the night, he stayed with Caryn alongside the platoon. "Glad you were along," he told her. "The women listened to you."

"It's a kind of understanding," she said and reached out and touched his arm. The moon was approaching the midnight sky when they returned to the field camp, where they found Miles waiting for them.

"We had two visits from war parties. I sent a squad out to meet each of them but they rode away," the general told Fargo.

"They were just looking, making sure you were all here," Fargo said. "There's not much time left. We'll go over plans for tomorrow night come morning. I need some shut-eye." Miles nodded, and one of the troopers took the Ovaro to the stables and Caryn came to Fargo's tent as he undressed.

"I want to go with you when you get the settlers tomorrow night," she said.

"Fine. I won't be taking the full platoon. I'll go over things with Miles tomorrow afternoon. Sit in on it," Fargo said.

She came forward and kissed him; it was no quick brush of her lips this time but a lingering, soft touch. "Find a time, a place, before hell breaks loose," she said.

"It won't be easy," he said.

"I still have confidence in you," she said and hurried away. He slept at once, tiredness taking charge of his body, but he awoke with the new day and washed and dressed hurriedly. At the stable, the Ovaro was groomed and waiting and he rode from the camp as the sun rose. He rode south, then after going west he doubled back and searched the plains until he found the lookouts. They were still in place, each carefully positioned to scan a given area. He knew that for each one he spotted there was another he didn't see. But in a perverse way he welcomed those he saw. They meant he had another twenty-four hours, another day of reprieve. The sun rose high, burning the prairie with heat waves, and finally he made his way back toward the camp. But he rode into the land that stretched out from the shoes of the river.

He rode the Ovaro slowly, making careful note of the small, isolated stands of trees that rose up some few hundred yards from the river and the camp. He took note of each, the first a small cluster of black oak, then, a hundred yards on, a stand of cottonwood. Closer to the river a group of staghorn sumac rose and further on, near the other end of the camp, another stand of black oak. They were all individual stands, none capable of harboring even a dozen horsemen, to say nothing of a full company. Fargo nodded approvingly. The Pawnee would see that at once and ignore the small tree clusters. Finally, he made his way into the camp, past the long line of tents and to the command tent, where the general waited. "Saw you upland. What were you looking for?" Miles asked.

"One-man hiding places," he said as the lieutenant entered, Caryn at his heels. "Let's talk about tonight. Have everybody ready to move out when I get back with the settlers."

"The entire company?" Miles asked.

"Including you." Fargo nodded. "First thing, they ride with stirrup leather pulled up and rein chains wrapped. The Pawnee won't see in the dark but they'll hear. They sleep like the cougar, always partly awake. The slap of stirrup leather and the rattle of rein chains of an entire company will damn well wake them."

"I'll see that everything's buttoned down," the lieutenant said.

"Next thing is you leave every tent just where it is. I want the Pawnee to think everybody's here and asleep. I don't want a thing out of place," Fargo said.

"Won't they notice the horses aren't tethered outside?" the general asked.

"No, because they'll be outside," Fargo said, half smiling at the general's surprised frown. "I've got it all down. Trust me," Fargo said. Turning to the lieutenant, he said, "I'll take you, Caryn, and six troopers to bring in the settlers. We start in an hour so we get to the settlers at dark. It'll take a while to bring them together."

"Stirrups pulled up and rein chains wrapped," Horgan said.

"Right. Six men is a lot different than a full company. We might get by but why take chances," Fargo said. "See you outside." Caryn followed him and stayed as he bound the stirrups up on her army mount and wrapped the rein chains in cloth. He had finished by the time Lieutenant Horgan approached with six troopers.

"You're not touching the Ovaro?" she asked.

"I can ride without slapping stirrup leather and my horse will respond to a rope halter for anything but hard riding," he said. He climbed onto the Ovaro and she rode beside him as the lieutenant and his troopers followed. He rode onto the high plains, staying at the edge of a line of burr oak. Night fell soon after he reached the Eberman cabin. "Send a trooper to each of the other families. Bring them here," he told Horgan, who rode off at once. "Stay at a walk," he called after the soldiers.

"The Bransons are bringing their wagon," Tom Eberman said. "Their little ones are too young to ride alone. We figured we'd all ride together."

"How many little ones?" Fargo asked.

"Three," Eberman said.

"But the Harrimans have two small ones," Clara Eberman put in. "And the Howarths have two."

"Each of the troopers will take one," Fargo said.

"I'll ride one," Caryn said.

"Wagon wheels squeak," Fargo said to Eberman. "You'll leave your animals and the Bransons will leave their wagon. It'll make things look normal here." Eberman agreed with a resigned nod and the other families began to arrive, each with a trooper. They were all on hand finally, the small children taken by Caryn and the troopers, and the line began to move slowly and silently through the night, across the high plains, and down toward the river. None of the settlers glanced back and none of them spoke. The children caught the tension in the air and also stayed silent, even the littlest ones.

Fargo led the procession, Caryn beside him, holding a four-year-old in front of her. He turned right only when they were directly up from the field camp and when he led the way past the double rows of pup tents he saw General Davis move out to meet him. The general had the full company in the saddle and waiting, he noted, and the moon hadn't reached the midnight sky. "We need some extra mounts," Fargo said. "I wouldn't let them bring their wagons."

"No problem," Miles said and relayed orders to a sergeant. Fargo waited until the extra horses were brought and everybody was in the saddle before turning back to Miles.

"We ride in the river. The horses will walk where it's shallow enough, swim where it isn't," Fargo said.

"In the river," Miles repeated, nodding as a wry smile of admiration crossed his face. "No hoofprints. Very clever. A trailsman's mind. But what about when we reach the Smoky Hills?"

"No hoofprints," he said enigmatically, and Miles nodded in acceptance. "Single file. Walk your horses. No talking," Fargo said.

"Pass the word," Miles told a sergeant.

"Let's move," Fargo said and led the way into the river, Caryn riding behind him, the settlers mixed in with the long line of troopers. The river remained shallow for a long stretch, the Ovaro's hooves touching the river bottom with ease. When the river grew deeper, the horse settled into a steady paddle and swam until the water grew shallow again. Fargo glanced back when he reached the end of a long curve, his eyes moving over the line of riders behind him. He watched the horses and their riders push slowly through the water with not even the faintest slap of stirrup leather, not the rattle of a rein chain. It seemed a ghostly procession in the pale of the moon, eerily silent, but Fargo nodded approvingly.

He refused to hurry as he led the strange parade through the winding river, and the moon was halfway across the night sky when he saw the dark outlines of the buttes and hills of the Smoky Mountains at his left. He let the long line come into shallow water before he raised an arm and called a halt. "Everybody dismount," he said. "Leave your horses and go ashore." There was a murmur of surprise mixed with uncertainty but they all followed the general as he left his horse and waded through the water to the shore. When they were all on the edge of the shore, Fargo faced them from the Ovaro. "You'll go due north on foot, into the Smoky Hills, and the land just back of the first row of buttes. There are plenty of caves, draws, rocks, and tree cover for everyone to hide. By dawn, I expect every one of you to be holed in somewhere. You're to stay there until you get word to come out. I expect the Indians will take the warpath in another twenty-four hours, maybe thirty-six. Ten troopers will take tree branches and smooth the ground after you and themselves so there won't be footprints." He paused to scan the upturned faces slowly. "There's a damn good chance they won't even come into the hills looking. But we can't count on that. You have to stay hidden or you're dead. Believe me."

"Where will you be, Fargo?" one of the settlers asked.

"Watching the field camp and the Pawnee attack. I'll need four troopers to take all the horses back upriver to the camp. I want them there," Fargo said.

"I'll have our mounts tethered in four lines," the lieutenant said.

"Five. I'll take one," Fargo said and Horgan stepped away to pick his troopers. Fargo addressed the others one more time. "If it goes the way I've planned, I'll be coming back for you. The real fighting will start then," he said.

"I'm going back with you," Caryn said.

"Get a pistol for her," Fargo said, and Miles handed

her his six-shot, single-action army-issue Colt. She came alongside Fargo as the troopers brought him the end of the tether, the horses strung out behind it. "Stay holed up, no matter what you hear," Fargo said again and began to lead the string of horses upriver. The four troopers fell in behind, each leading another string of mounts. Caryn beside him, he kept the same slow and silent pace as he rode back upriver and the night still hung at the edge of dawn when he reached the tents of the now-deserted field camp. The troopers tethered all the horses where they were usually tethered. Fargo watched them as the first streaks of dawn touched the horizon.

"We'll never make it back to the hills before daylight," one of the troopers said.

"Didn't expect that, didn't want that," Fargo said. "Fact is, you won't get very far from here before it's light. There's plenty of good tree cover big enough for four horses up from the other side of the river. Pick one and hole up inside it. Comes day, and maybe comes tomorrow, you just stay put and watch the river. When you see me, you come out. Not before. Understood, soldier?" Fargo said.

"Understood, sir," the trooper said and the other three followed him as he rode down through the river to disappear in the dark. Fargo turned the Ovaro up the gentle slope that led away from the river and the camp. In the near day he peered at the small clusters of trees he had staked out, two black oaks, one cottonwood, and one staghorn sumac. The sumac wasn't far enough from the river, he decided, the cottonwoods too open at the bottom. He chose the nearest of the black oak, nosing the pinto deep into the denseness of the trees, and dismounted. He motioned to Caryn to tie her mount to the low branch beside the Ovaro. Setting out his bedroll as dawn began to roll away the night, he lay down on it on his stomach and peered out through the thick foliage. Caryn came down to lay beside him.

The field camp tents along both sides of the river were exactly as they always were. The unsaddled army horses were tethered in four groups as usual. The scene appeared completely as usual and he let out a grunt of satisfaction. "Now what?" Caryn asked.

"We get some sleep," he said. "Nothing's going to happen real soon."

"Sleep. That's an appealing thought," she said and shed her clothes as he did. Warm and soft, she lay against him and was asleep in seconds. He closed his eyes as the sun rose across the prairie as it did every morning, as if the day would be just like every other day.

8

The sun had passed the noon sky when he awoke.
Caryn opened her eyes beside him. The day was hot,
even inside the tree-covered bower where they lay, and
he watched her get up and go to her horse and come
back with her canteen. She sat down beside him, every
movement gracefully beautiful, her long waist sinuous,
her body swaying with its own smoothness, and he
watched the way her breasts dipped and rose and
dipped again as she used the cool water of the canteen
to wash. It took an effort for him to pull his eyes from
her and go to the Ovaro and wash out of his own canteen. When he finished, he pulled on his clothes while
she was still beautifully naked. "You figure to stay that
way all day?" he asked.

"Why not? I'm not going anywhere," she said. "It's
nice and cool this way."

"Be back soon," he said.

"Where are you going?" she asked apprehensively.

"Down to the camp. If they're watching it'll let
them see some activity," he said. "I'll fill the canteens,
maybe find something to eat in the mess tent." She sat
back on her elbows, her breasts thrust upward insou-
ciantly, their flat, pale pink tips little-girl-like.

"Hurry back," she said.

"Count on it," he answered as he took the Ovaro

and walked the horse out at the back of the cluster of trees before swinging into the saddle. He circled and rode east, approaching the tents of the camp from the far end. He rummaged through the mess tent, found fresh water barrels, and filled the canteens. He also came upon some jam and biscuits that were relatively fresh and an end of dried ham hock, enough for a meal. He stuffed his finds into his saddlebag and rode the pinto to the river's edge, sending it to casually saunter across to the other side and then to idly wander along the plains. But there was no idle casualness to the lake blue eyes that squinted over the sage from the wide brim of the Stetson. They swept the near land and the distant reaches and finally he turned the horse, crossed the river again, and rode east.

He stayed east until he was far beyond the camp, then turned north up the slope that led from the river, and circled back to the cluster of black oak, entering the trees from the back side. Caryn was sitting up, and he smiled at the incongruousness of her as she sat naked with the army Colt raised in one hand. "Just me," he said as he pushed through the trees and she lowered the pistol. He swung from the horse, tied the reins to a branch, and brought the food to her where she sat atop the bedroll. "No more lookouts," he said as he lowered himself down beside her.

Her eyes searched his face gravely. "The time's come," she said.

"Dawn, I'd guess. They'll hit when they think everybody's still asleep or just waking."

"Dawn," she echoed, her lips pursing. "Less than a day or more than a lifetime. Take your pick."

"Don't think I'll pick either," he said as they shared the food he'd brought and the sun slid toward the horizon. When they finished, she put everything left away and began to unbutton his shirt. He let her take his clothes off as he enjoyed the beauty of her. He felt himself responding to her touch and finally he was naked with her and pulled her to him. She brought the sweet, high breasts to his mouth, pushed first one, then the other, to his lips and as he pulled on the flat, pale pink nipples he could feel them blossom under his tongue. "Ah, ah, yes . . . oh, God, yes," she murmured as he caressed her, gently sucking and pulling harder as her cries rose. The narrow waist twisted, rose and fell back. Her hands slid up and down his back, digging into his skin making little paths with her nails.

She fell back and he went with her, his hard-muscled frame lying over her, his throbbing erectness pressed down over her modest V and she gasped out half words. He felt her hand reaching, searching, and he moved and let her find him. "Oh my God, oh, please, please," she cried out and he half turned as she held him, stroking, pulling, clasping, fondling, and making little sounds of delight. She pulled on him as her hips pushed upward and he went with her, letting her bring him to her. He felt the warm dampness of the inside of her long thighs as she touched him. "Take me, Fargo, oh take me, take me, take me." A wild cry rose from her as he moved with her, letting the tip of his pulsating warmness touch the lubricous walls and slide forward.

"Oh . . . ooooooh," Caryn moaned and pushed forward to take all of him, screaming out when he touched the very end of the dark, honeyed tunnel, exploding in a sudden paroxysm of quivering, trembling movements. Her thighs clasped hard against him as she pushed and thrust with him, her arms circling his neck, pulling his face down to her breasts. "Yes, yes,

yes. More, more, more," she screamed out as he enjoyed every instant of her. He could feel the ecstasy sweep through him at her total enjoyment. She clasped him to her, moved with him, rolled with him, clinging and rubbing until it seemed she was trying to make herself one with him. Her smooth, silken skin grew warm, covered with a thin coating of perspiration that not only let her slide her body against his but somehow heightened the wild eroticism of their lovemaking. Finally, he felt her honeyed walls tightening around him, sweet, wonderful sensations, and Caryn screamed, sound and substance erupting as one, the spirit and the senses joining in an explosion of ecstasy.

She stayed tight against him as her screams and gasps slowly subsided, her quivering body growing still and the ultimate pleasure slipping into reluctant memory. "Stay, stay," she whispered as she held him inside her and he remained with her, enjoying the wet warmth of her encompassing him. Finally, she relaxed and fell away, turning to lie half over him, one long lovely thigh across his groin. Dusk had come to the land, he noted as he cradled one high breast to him. She caught him glancing through the trees and smiled, a slightly smug smile. "The night's young," she murmured. He nodded and held her tighter.

She half slept with him and night came and the moon managed to filter its pale light through the trees, enough for him to enjoy the beauty of her as her skin turned milk white in the moon's glow and the pale pink nipples became ghostly little points that remained terribly attractive. He let himself doze with her and when they woke, her long-waisted body slid against him and she needed no words to spell out wanting. They made love again, and then later in the night, once again. But everything slower, now, the first, wild frenzy of her turned into long and languorous desire. He enjoyed the touch and taste of every part of her, from the little-girl nipples to the very womanly, fibrous nap, slowly feeling and caressing all the secret, warm places of her as she cried out little sounds of delight. With her he immersed himself in the sensuous, the most intimate, complete pleasure of every bodily sense and the night became a wonderful place where all else was shut out.

Subconsciously, they both denied tomorrow, reveling in their escape. There are all kinds of ways to protect yourself, he reflected later. This was one of the best. But finally he slept with her until the warm night neared an end. The clock inside him went off and he rose in the last hanging minutes of the night and gently shook her awake. She blinked and slid her arms around him, her breasts touching his chest. "I'm tempted to say I don't care about today," she murmured.

"Don't," he said.

"I won't. Truth is, I care more now."

"More?"

"I want tonight to come again, and again," she said.

"Get dressed," he told her gently and she pulled on her clothes as he did. They were both dressed, the bedroll put away, and she lay beside him on her stomach as he peered through the curtain of leaves. Day was chasing away the last of the night, the double rows of tents taking shape alongside the river. Fargo strained his ears to listen but the shapes took form soundlessly and he saw they were moving on foot, leading their horses. His eyes swept the plain and he cursed silently. The Indians seemed to cover the prairie sagebrush and as the light increased he could make out the tall, thin figure at the head of the horse.

At a signal from the chief they swung onto their ponies. At another signal, they charged forward as one, sweeping down on the field camp. No war whoops, he noted, no high-pitched cries of attack. They wanted surprise, complete and total, and he allowed himself a grim smile. They'd have their surprise, but not the one they expected. He felt Caryn's hand tighten on his arm as the Pawnee reached the camp and split into two lines, one attacking the first set of tents, the other the second. They poured rifle fire and arrows into the tents as they raced past each. Then they turned and raced by again with another volley of fire. A third band of near-naked riders attacked each row of tents from the front, again pouring arrows and gunfire into each tent, raking their targets with a wicked cross fire.

Fargo found the Pawnee chief where he had halted off to one side with another four chiefs. Raising his hand high in the air, Tall Tree signaled his warriors and they pulled back, drawing to a halt. Every heavy-featured face peered at the tents, each frowning as it became clear no one had answered the attack. The chief signaled again and a dozen braves detached themselves from the main force. They approached the first line of tents, this time slowly, cautiously. They spread out when they reached the tents, and leaning from their ponies, they used their rifles to carefully lift the tent flaps. In moments, shouts of surprise and anger echoed to where Fargo and Caryn lay in the cluster of oaks. More Pawnee moved to the other tents and more shouts of surprise followed. They called to the chief and Fargo saw the Pawnee leader explode in a torrent of fury, shouting commands, gesticulating wildly.

Half the warriors stayed in place but the other half

raced off in every direction, leaning from their mounts, their eyes searching the ground. "Looking for hoofprints," Fargo whispered to Caryn. A dozen riders climbed the slow slope toward the oaks where they lay. He watched as the Indians rode in a crisscross pattern, sweeping the ground with their angry glances. Four riders came directly toward the cluster of black oaks. They scanned the clump of trees and those nearby. Fargo felt the dryness inside his mouth and hoped he had guessed right as he saw the riders slow, peer at the trees, and then move on. The small cluster of trees couldn't hold any sizeable group of soldiers and their mounts and the Pawnee concluded as much as the four braves moved out of his line of vision. He let a deep breath pass through his lips as he waited. Three of the four braves reappeared, passed by, and turned down the slope.

The fourth one had apparently gone off on his own and again Fargo let relief surge through him. He had guessed right. The Pawnee had concluded that the tree clusters were too small to hide troops. He watched the others rejoin the main body of the Pawnee beside the river as the other searchers began to return, plainly angry and frustrated. He was about to shift his position when he caught the sound from the rear of the oaks, the soft thud of an unshod pony coming to a halt. Caryn caught the sound, too, and her eyes grew wide with fear as she glanced at him.

He put his lips to her ear, his whisper barely audible even then. "No shots. They'll hear them below. This has to be quick and silent." She nodded and Fargo turned his body as he peered into the rear of the oaks and saw the branches move. The Pawnee had dropped from his pony and was probing his way on foot. Fargo heard the Indian drawing in deep breaths of air and he frowned. The figure was still hidden in the thick foliage as he advanced. He paused to draw in another deep breath. Caryn's lips touched Fargo's ear.

"Why is he breathing so hard?" she whispered.

"Goddamn," Fargo whispered back. "Goddamn."

"What kind of an answer's that?" she whispered back.

"He'll be here in minutes. When he gets here, you get up, let him see you," Fargo whispered and rolled away from her. Inching his way on the flat of his stomach, he pushed into the trees at his right, taking care not to rustle a blade of grass or move a leaf. He halted and lay silently, his eyes peering at Caryn. He saw her move and suddenly push to her feet, and the Pawnee came into his line of vision. Carrying a rifle, the Indian saw her and halted in surprise. He started toward her, holding the rifle with both hands across his bare chest. Caryn stayed in place and she didn't have to feign fear.

They were both only a half-dozen feet from where Fargo lay and he waited another ten seconds, letting the Indian take another step toward Caryn. "Come," the man barked in his language as Caryn just stared at him. Fargo gathered every muscle in his powerful calves and legs and pushed himself up on the palms of his hands. He dived forward and upward at the same time, becoming a missile hurtling through the air. The Indian turned, caught by surprise, his concentration still on Caryn.

His eyes widened and he started to bring the rifle up. He had it raised almost to the top of his chest when Fargo plowed into him. Seizing the rifle with both hands, Fargo drove it upward, under the man's chin and into his throat, all his power and weight behind it. The Indian made a hoarse, gasping noise as the rifle smashed into his larynx. He fell backward, still gasping for air. Fargo tore the rifle from his hands and brought the heavy stock down onto the man's forehead and heard the terrible cracking sound. The Pawnee hit the ground on his back and lay still, instantly limp. Fargo drew back and let the rifle fall to the ground. He was at Caryn's side in two long strides.

"Jesus," she murmured, clinging to him.

"Quick and quiet," he muttered. "He wasn't breathing hard. He was smelling hard, drawing in a scent, following his nose."

She frowned at him. "He smelled us from out behind the trees?"

"Not us," Fargo said grimly as he kicked the nearby sack and the piece of ham hock rolled out. "This, dammit. He smelled the ham. It alerted him instantly. He's a Pawnee. It was an odor that wasn't supposed to be there. My mistake. I didn't wrap it tight." He looked past her through the trees and down at the field camp. The Indians were beginning to move south along the river, some spreading out as they rode, but all moving southward. He spotted Tall Tree with four riders alongside him.

"What about the one here? Won't they miss him?" Caryn asked.

"Not for a day or two. There are too many out riding on their own," Fargo said.

"They're riding on land, not through the river as we did. They'll make better time. They'll reach the Smoky Hills before sundown," Caryn said. "What happens then?"

"If things were done right, they shouldn't find anything. They'll check out the hills, they won't go making a real search," Fargo said. "They'll figure everybody's running to make Fort Travis. They'll go after them."

"What happens when they don't catch up to them?" Caryn questioned.

"They'll wonder and decide they reached the fort," Fargo said as he lowered himself to the ground. He continued to peer out through the trees. The last of the Indian horsemen soon left his sight. "We wait here a spell, give them time to get plenty far downriver. Then we follow after them." Caryn sat down beside him and he saw the troubled furrow cling to her face. "What's bothering you?" he asked.

"I keep wondering what if it goes wrong. What if our people don't hide well? What if one of the settlers' little ones starts crying when the Pawnee are near? What happens then?" she said.

His face stiffened. There was nothing gained by shading the truth. "Pretty much of a massacre," he told her. "Inexperienced troops on foot against the Pawnee, Kiowa, Cheyenne, Osage, and Kansa on horseback."

"How will we know?" she asked.

"We'll know when we get there," he said. She said nothing and leaned back against a tree trunk and the quiet fear clung to her. He let another hour go by before he rose and untied the horses. "Time for finding out," he said and handed her the reins of her army mount. He pushed from the small cluster of oaks that had been their hiding place and swung onto the Ovaro. He started down the slope to the river, Caryn at his side. He passed the tents and rode the riverbank at a trot, making good time. He had gone more than a mile when they passed a long line of red cedar. When he caught the movement of leaves, the Colt was instantly in his hand.

He was ready to yank the horse into a tight circle when the figure came out of the trees and he saw the blue uniform with the gold edging. He reined to a halt and the three other troopers emerged from the trees. "They passed hours ago, riding hard," the trooper said. "We stayed holed up, wondering if you'd be coming by."

"Go back to the camp and get the horses. Bring them downriver. Stay in the river. I'll be waiting by the Smoky Hills," Fargo said. The trooper nodded and rode back toward the camp, the others at his heels. Fargo continued on along the bank and Caryn stayed beside him.

"Why did you have them ride through the river when we're taking the bank?" she asked.

"Pawnee scouts may double back. You never know. They won't pay attention to two horses. They will to a hundred," he said, increasing the pace, one eye on the sky, which was starting to turn gray. He pointed out the wide swath of unshod pony prints that covered both sides of the river and the day drew to a close as they rode on. The moon had risen high in the sky when they reached the Smoky Hills and Fargo slowed to a walk as he peered at the Pawnee tracks. The Indians had halted to explore the land that led into the hills, but Fargo let a deep sigh of relief escape his lips. The ground was not littered with bodies. His maneuver had worked and while Caryn waited, he explored further under the high moon, spotting where the Pawnee had finally gone on.

He returned to Caryn and she rode beside him as he slowly climbed into the hills, noting where the Pawnee had explored, and gone on past the buttes. He saw more pony prints under the moonlight, but not as many. They had crossed back and forth, their search cursory. When he reached the hills behind the buttes he halted. "General Miles Davis," he called out. "Coming out time." He repeated the call three times more before he caught movement at the mouth of a ravine. A figure stepped into sight and walked toward him. He saw the shock of white hair glow in the moonlight.

"By God, I've never been so glad to see anybody in my life," Miles said. Fargo's eyes went past the straight figure to see other figures emerging from the ravine, from small gullies, from out of hollow logs, and from behind trees and out of rocky defiles. He brought his eyes back to the general. "They came looking," Miles said. "But not too hard. They didn't see any footprints. They'd no reason to keep looking. It went just the way you hoped it would."

"Thank God for that," Fargo said.

"I could get a glimpse of them from where I was holed up. It's a powerful force," the general said. "They went on south, finally."

"On their way to Fort Travis. They've got to attack somebody. They've got to have a victory," Fargo said. He glanced past the general as the troopers crowded up, some of the settlers mixed in with them. Caryn glanced at a woman holding two small children.

"I was so afraid one of the children might cry when the Pawnee were looking," Caryn said.

"They were too afraid to cry," the woman said.

"Sometimes being scared comes in handy," Caryn said.

"Bring your weapons and start down to the river," Fargo said to the others. "No hurry. It'll be a spell before the horses get here." The general walked with him as he started back down to the river.

"You did it, Fargo," he said. "This much of it. The rest is up to my company and to me. But we'd all be dead if it hadn't worked the way you figured it would. You saw a way and made it happen."

"Everybody played a part in making it happen. As Caryn said, to the smallest child," Fargo said.

"It's a miracle it worked. So many things could have happened to blow it sky high," Miles said. "Any little, unexpected thing."

"Try a ham hock," Caryn said and the general frowned back.

"Some other time," Fargo said and was glad they had reached the river. The troopers lined the bank and the settlers and their families formed their own group. The moon was moving down to the end of the night sky when Fargo heard the soft lapping sound. He peered upriver and saw the first line of horses come into sight. The others followed closely and Lieutenant Horgan moved back and forth along the riverbank.

"Find your mounts," he said to the men, who pushed past each other to search out their horses. Fargo turned to the settlers.

"You'll take the extra horses you rode here. Go back to your homes. When this is over, the Pawnee will have had their share of attacking and killing. You'll be safe as you've ever been," he said.

"We can live with that," Tom Eberman said. "Maybe you'll come visit sometime. We'd all like that."

"We'll see when it's over," he said. A trooper brought the extra horses to Eberman and Fargo saw that the full company had taken their saddles. Miles climbed onto his mount and threw Fargo a glance.

"Nobody's had any real sleep. I'd like the men to get some before they take on the Pawnee and the others," the general said.

"We'll ride till sunup, find some shade, and sleep till midmorning," Fargo said.

"That'll be enough," Miles said and led the company forward. The soldiers automatically fell into two columns of twos and Fargo brought up the rear with Caryn.

"I feel like it should be an end," she said. "But it's only a beginning. The real fighting's still ahead of us." He didn't answer. There was no need. "I hope it goes as well as this did," she said.

"That'd be nice," he agreed blandly and she threw a sharp glance at him. He leaned over, closed a hand around her shoulder for a moment, and rode on. A large forest of hackberry rose up ahead of the riders as the sun appeared. He followed the company into the shade of the forest, found a spot for himself and Caryn, and set out his bedroll. They both slept at once and he woke with the others at midmorning. A small tributary of the river let the men refresh themselves and the horses drink. When they prepared to move forward, Fargo and Caryn rode up alongside Lieutenant Horgan and just back of the general. "There's a good stand of trees back from the fort," he said to Horgan. "That'll let us get in a little closer before we hit the open land. If I'm right, the Pawnee will still be concentrating on the fort. That could give us a little more time to surprise them."

"The general hasn't given us any orders yet," the lieutenant said.

"Orders?" Fargo echoed.

"Like whether he wants us to execute a flanking maneuver and come at them from the sides," Horgan said. "I think that'd be a good idea, really take them by surprise."

"You ever execute a flanking maneuver?" Fargo asked.

"Only in training," the lieutenant said. "But it's an option I'm sure he's considering."

"Yes, of course," Fargo said and caught Caryn's eye

as he kept his face expressionless. She dropped back and he went with her as she knew he would.

"Say it, whatever you're thinking," she hissed at him.

"The general doesn't have any options to consider," he said to her. "He has a company of inexperienced kids and that doesn't allow for options."

"What about the lieutenant's idea, a flanking maneuver?" she persisted.

"A flanking maneuver against the Indians by a company of troops who've never done one for real?" Fargo grimaced. "The Indians are masters of the flanking movement, how to execute one and how to get out of one."

"What do you think Miles will do?" she asked.

"Let them fight and try to stop them from making bad moves," Fargo said and fell silent. The sun had crossed the midafternoon sky and he saw the land grow heavier with tree cover. "We'll reach the fort in a few more minutes," he said.

"I'm ready," Caryn said.

"You're going to stay in the trees, out of sight," he said and drew an instant frown.

"I didn't come here for that. I didn't come here to hide," she said.

"I know you didn't, but that's what I want you to do," Fargo said. "I want you out of sight in the trees. I don't want anyone to see you."

"I want to get inside that fort. There's a man there who arranged to have me killed. I want to face him," Caryn insisted.

"You will, but my way," Fargo said adamantly.

"Promise?" she thrust at him.

"Promise," he said. She glowered, letting thoughts turn inside her and finally letting her lips relax.

"All right," she agreed. He left her and rode past the lieutenant to where Miles was just reining his mount to a halt.

"The fort's on the clear land just the other side of those trees," the general said. "Haven't seen any signs of Indians so I'm guessing they're still attacking the fort. Sounds a terrible thing to say but I hope so."

"I know what you mean," Fargo said.

"The only good thing about this is that Cogwell will be real embarrassed to have the Secretary of the Army in his fort under attack. He didn't expect this, you can be sure of that," Miles said.

"I'm sure he didn't but he'll turn it his way. He'll use it to show how you weren't able to stop your company from being wiped out," Fargo said.

"Probably," Miles said glumly. Then he turned his horse and rode to where he could face the line of troops. "We're going into battle. When the bugler sounds the attack, Platoons A and B respond. Only Platoons A and B," he emphasized. "At the next call, everybody goes. There'll be no fancy maneuvers, no textbook tactics. My orders are very simple. Go out there and shoot anything that wears a loincloth. God be with every one of you."

He turned, waved an arm, and led the company into the forest of hackberry. Fargo rode alongside him with Caryn, the journey through the trees short and direct. Rifle fire suddenly became a staccato rhythm overlaid with war whoops. The last of the trees came into view. Fargo moved almost to the edge of the last line of trees, halted, and looked at Caryn. "This is the end of the line for you," he said. She stared back, her lips tight. "You agreed," he reminded her.

"I'll stay," she muttered. "You made a promise."

"I'll keep it," he said. If I'm around to keep it, he murmured inwardly and moved the Ovaro forward.

9

Fargo halted at the last of the hackberry as the general stopped and turned to the bugler beside him. Fargo peered through the trees. There had been a number of settlements just outside the fort. Now they were marked by the bodies that littered the ground. They had silent company clothed in cavalry uniforms. Too much company. It was clear that the Indians had struck fast and hard, taking the fort by complete surprise. But the defenders had pulled the gates closed, he saw. His eyes moved to the battle that was going on in front of him.

Two lines of attackers raced back and forth, one lofted a steady hail of arrows into the fort over the top of the stockade walls. The other were riflemen that sent bullets at the soldiers that leaped up to fire over the walls. Fargo saw a half-dozen knots of Pawnee trying to set fire to the base of the stockade with twigs and fire arrows. Defenders inside the fort fired down at them and ducked the rifle fire from the racing riders. But the attackers had not had everything their own way. They'd left a number of bodies outside the fort, he saw. The general's voice broke into his survey.

"Sound charge," Miles barked. The bugle's clarion call resounded through the trees and Fargo saw Platoons A and B charge forward. At the fort the attackers whirled in surprise and tried to gather themselves, but the troopers fired off a barrage as they charged. Fargo saw a number of Pawnee go down from the first barrage. The Pawnee on their ponies responded in their usual way, racing off in all directions, skidding to a halt, and returning to fire back in a half circle. They broke off again, raced away, and returned from all directions. In moments the troopers were no longer charging, but defending themselves, their initial attack blunted. It had quickly become a pitched battle with riders going down on both sides. Fargo threw a glance at Miles but the general sat impassively, his eyes narrowed at the battle going on. Fargo had a moment of uncertainty go through his mind. Miles was letting the two platoons sustain too many casualties, since their inexperience prevented them from properly meeting the Pawnee's tactics.

Suddenly the air filled with new, high-pitched cries and Fargo saw two large groups of loin-clothed riders converge on the troopers from both sides, racing around both sides of the fort. When he noticed Tall Tree to the side, he realized this was the main part of the Indian force. There was no uncertainty in the glance he threw at Miles this time, only a nod of understanding and approval as the general barked commands and the bugle blared forth again. The trees shook with the rush of horses sent into a gallop as the remainder of the full company charged into the battle.

Miles had suspected the Indians would hold back. He had trumped them at their own tactics. The troopers struck and the Pawnee main force circled, taken by surprise. The pitched battle had grown bigger and had spread out in all directions. The troopers were doing better than he'd expected. He drew the Colt at his hip and sent the Ovaro racing forward into the open. A half-dozen braves flew past in front of him. Only four made it to where they were headed. He drew a bead on a brave with a Cheyenne armband who had knocked a trooper from his horse and stood over him with tomahawk raised. Fargo fired and the Cheyenne staggered backward, the tomahawk falling from his hands. He crumpled to the ground as the trooper regained his feet. He flashed Fargo a glance of gratitude from a pale-cheeked face. Fargo ducked as he heard the horse coming up at his right. He felt the tomahawk sail over his head and started to bring the Colt up to fire at the Indian who raced by when he felt the rush of air at his other side.

He ducked instinctively, and the Indian's dive didn't hit him fully in the back. Yet the blow was enough to send him over the side of the Ovaro. Twisting as best he could as he fell, he managed to hit the ground on his side. When he turned he saw the Pawnee standing, bringing his tomahawk down in a sweeping blow. There weren't enough seconds for him to roll away without the short-handled ax plunging into him. Instead, he flung himself against the Pawnee and hit the man at the ankles. The Indian lost his balance, the tomahawk missing its mark as his legs went out from under him. He tried to stop himself from falling completely forward but Fargo fired from his prone position underneath the Indian. The bullet traveled straight upward, striking the man under his jaw and traveling up to almost split his head in two.

Fargo rolled away as the figure collapsed in a shower of scarlet. Pushing to his feet, Fargo spied the Ovaro a few paces away. He ran for the horse and reloaded at the same time. Vaulting into the saddle, he was just in time to send another Cheyenne flying from his pony. Staying low in the saddle, Fargo managed a moment to take in the scene. Bodies seemed to almost cover the

137

ground, yet Indians and troopers still found space to ride and fire. With surprise, Fargo saw that the troopers were more than holding their own with help from others firing from the top of the stockade. The attackers were by no means wiped out but they'd been hit hard. Fargo swept the scene and he saw Tall Tree to one side with a small knot of warriors. As he spied the Pawnee chief, he saw the Indian pump one long arm up and down twice, wheeling his horse and starting to race away.

The others immediately broke off the battle and began to gallop after the chief. A half dozen more fell as troopers poured fire after them. A few turned on their ponies and fired back with rifles and arrows and three troopers went down. Some started to race after the fleeing Indians and Fargo spurred the Ovaro forward, cutting in front of them. "No," he shouted. "Don't give chase. They'll come around and catch you in a cross fire." The troopers slowed and hesitated.

"Listen to the man," a voice shouted and Fargo saw Horgan come up. "Disengage and dismount. See to the wounded."

Fargo nodded at the lieutenant and sent the Ovaro after the Pawnee. He had unfinished business to see to. He saw the Indians had slowed and had gathered into separate clusters as they moved along the open land between a line of serviceberry and one of cottonwoods. Fargo swerved, sent the Ovaro to the left, and stayed by the cottonwoods, managing to gain on the Pawnee while staying parallel to the center force. He was quickly gaining ground and was almost abreast of the Indians when the three riders burst from the trees. The first one wore a neck band with the unmistakable markings of the Kiowa. Fargo immediately swerved the Ovaro into the trees and turned in a circle inside the forest as the three Kiowa came back into the forest after him. But he had halted and waited, peering through the branches, where he spotted the three riders moving carefully.

All carried rifles, he saw, and he raised the Colt, measuring distances. He had no time to toy with the three pursuers, Fargo reminded himself, no time to offer them a chance to back off. It was unlikely they would, he told himself. They'd show him no mercy. He had no choice but to return the dubious favor. The Colt raised to fire, he let the three men move forward until they were all in his direct line of fire. He wondered if one bullet aimed perfectly might not bring down all three, hurtling through one, then the other, and finally the third. His lips pulled back as he discarded the thought. The odds were no good and this was not a time to play bad odds.

The Kiowa moved closer and Fargo steadied his hand against the saddle horn and fired, three shots triggered so fast that the sounds overlapped each other. The three figures toppled from their horses as if they were a trio of puppets pulled by a single string. Fargo spurred the pinto into a gallop and burst from the trees to see a line of Pawnee coming at him. Another quick glance showed him Tall Tree, some fifty yards on with a lone rider at his side. Fargo spun the Ovaro back into the cottonwoods but kept the horse at a gallop and raced through the trees. The line of horsemen would come in after he had had a good start and the Ovaro was expert at cutting through trees without losing speed. A sturdy, powerful rump and quick turning ability were his secrets.

When Fargo swerved the horse to the left once more and sped out of the forest, he'd gone some hundred yards. He raced across open land to cut off the Pawnee chief, skidding the Ovaro to a halt directly in the Indian's path. He glanced at the rider alongside Tall Tree and saw it was the courier and interpreter. The main force of Indians were a ways back but quickly headed toward the chief. They wouldn't count, not now, Fargo felt certain. He straightened the Ovaro to face the Pawnee chief. Tall Tree walked his pony slowly forward and started to bring up his rifle. Fargo recognized it as one of the Winchesters taken from Bart Whitman. Pulling the big Henry from its saddlecase, Fargo leveled it at the tall figure who sat ramrod straight on his pony.

He faced the chief, less than ten yards separating him from the Indian, both with rifles aimed directly at each other. Fargo knew he'd not miss. The Pawnee hadn't handled a Winchester long enough to be a crack shot with one. But at this distance he'd not miss, either. "It did not go your way," Fargo said over the barrel of the Henry.

The chief frowned as the interpreter translated. "You think you have won? You fool yourself," he said.

"No. We haven't won. But you wanted a great victory. You have not won it," Fargo said.

Tall Tree frowned at him. "Because of you," he said and the other Indian translated again. "I know this inside me. I feel it. You. I do not know how or why but it was you." Fargo said nothing. The main body of the Pawnee halted in a wide half circle, looking on as they listened. "And now you think a Pawnee chief will tremble before your gun?" Tall Tree said, keeping his rifle raised and steady as a rock.

"No, I don't think that," Fargo said.

"We will exchange bullets and exchange deaths. Have you come for that?" the chief said.

"No," Fargo said. "I came to talk of another way."

"Your other way is no good. A great chief will never lead his people in the way that is wrong. You do not understand this," the Pawnee said.

"I understand that," Fargo said.

"Prove it," Tall Tree said. "A great chief is forever a great chief. Nothing can change that. It is written so. Say you know this and we can go our ways."

Fargo's thoughts raced. It was a challenge. It would humble him in front of all the others. It was also a way out of an impasse. More than that, it was the chance Fargo wanted, the chance to do what he'd come to do. "A chief's daughter is forever a chief's daughter. Nothing can change that. It is written so. Say you know this," he tossed back. The chief's eyes narrowed as they peered at him.

"You are like a white buffalo, strange and different," the Pawnee said.

"Say you know this and we will go our ways," Fargo echoed.

"I say this." The chief nodded. "And say you?"

"What you have asked," Fargo answered. He saw the barrel of the Winchester begin to lower and he brought the Henry down and started to turn away on the Ovaro.

"Till another time," the chief said. "Do you understand?"

Fargo nodded at the words that were a vow, admission without concession, an affirmation that there would be, at best, a hiatus and nothing more. Hate had not vanished. Obsessions had not changed. Emnity had not lessened. But a daughter was restored. Perhaps it would be the only good to come out of it all, Fargo pondered and let himself take comfort in that.

He slowly pushed his way through the silent warriors. Leaving them behind, he turned east toward Fort Travis. Another daughter waited there. Two fathers, two daughters, a parallel that was not really a parallel. The Pawnee chief had his principles. They were there despite his unyielding stiffness, despite his obsessions and hate. Honor was personal, its own code. He would abide by it. Herbert Cogwell had no code except his own ambition. He had neither principles nor honor. It would not turn out as well for Caryn. A measure of satisfaction was all she could hope for. Would it be enough for her, he wondered.

His lips drew back in a grimace. He reached the fort with uneasiness wrapping itself tighter around him. He saw they had set up rows of stretchers outside, most with sheets covering them. But there were other rows of men being tended to and bandaged. He paused at the cottonwoods and Caryn came forward at once. "I've done enough waiting," she said. "And worrying about you."

"A few minutes more. I'll be sending for you," he said. She frowned and finally agreed with a nod. He rode on and found Miles and the general. Detaching himself from a cluster of bandaged troopers, Fargo asked, "You see Cogwell?"

"He's inside with Secretary Elliman," Miles said. "You've some kind of plan laid out, don't you?"

"Yes, I want to give him the chance to dig his own hole deeper before he's confronted," Fargo said. As he walked toward the command building at the center of the fort, Miles beside him, he spied Lieutenant Roswall and Lieutenant Horgan. He beckoned and both young officers hurried over. "You two are going to wait right outside the door while Miles and I go inside. I'll be calling on both of you when the time comes. You'll be first, Horgan. Caryn Cogwell's waiting in the first cluster of trees. When I tell you, you go get her and fast," Fargo said.

"Yes, sir," the young officer said.

Fargo turned to Roswall. "You'll step inside when I call you. You'll just tell the truth of it, no holding back," Fargo said.

"I'll like that," Roswall said. The two junior officers halted as Fargo and Miles reached the large interior of the main room of the fort. He saw Howard Elliman, his face white and shaken, seated beside a heavy desk, General Cogwell standing near him. Cogwell held an expression of smugness on his face, turned as Fargo entered with General Davis. The smugness vanished, replaced by shock, first, then wariness, then alarm.

"What are you doing here?"

"Unfinished business," Fargo said. "I'll let General Davis start."

Miles Davis faced Cogwell, ice wreathing his face. "You're finished, Cogwell, once and for all," he said. He turned to the Secretary of the Army, and suddenly there was thunder in his voice. "I charge General Cogwell with being a liar, a provocateur, a disgrace to his uniform, a traitor to his commission, and an attempted murderer. Maybe that shouldn't be attempted. Maybe it should be murderer. I ask that he be put in irons and held for a full military trial."

Elliman stared back with his jaw dropping open. He looked at Cogwell and back to Miles Davis again. Cogwell's shout cut into the moment.

"This man's come unhinged. He's in some kind of battle shock. I've seen it happen before," Cogwell said.

"Shock is right but not battle shock," Miles said. "Shock at an officer who, to further his own ambitions, stirred up the Pawnee so they'd take to the warpath in a major uprising. Shock at a man who arranged for me to have nothing but young, inexperienced troops, then purposely held back my request for reinforcements so my command would be wiped out. That's what would have happened if Fargo hadn't found a way to prevent it."

Howard Elliman stared at Cogwell, a frown on his brow. "He's gone completely mad," Cogwell said with a snarl at Miles.

Miles put a hand on Fargo's shoulder. "This is Skye Fargo. You can thank him for being alive, Mr. Secretary. He'll back up everything I've said."

"He's a scout for Davis, in his pay. He's nothing but an adventurer. You can't believe him," Cogwell protested.

"And adventurer known as the Trailsman with the finest reputation in the West," Miles said.

Elliman peered at Fargo. "The Trailsman. Yes, I've heard the name. President Buchanan had you work for him once, I believe," the man said.

"Bull's-eye," Fargo said.

"Fargo saw my request for reinforcements in General Cogwell's files two months after I sent it," Miles said.

"Is that right?" Elliman asked Fargo.

"Yes, sir," Fargo said.

"He was mistaken. He saw something else," Cogwell put in.

"Hell I did," Fargo threw back.

Elliman turned to look hard at Cogwell and Fargo saw the uncertainty that had come into the man's face. Elliman didn't want to believe the accusations that had been flung but now there were two accusers and Cogwell was showing signs of panic. Suddenly there was at least the long shadow of substance and Howard Elliman was a confused and uncomfortable man. Fargo leaned out the doorway to where Horgan waited next to Roswall. "Get her," he whispered and Horgan took off running. Fargo pulled back and returned his attention to

Elliman. "I can back up what I said and what I saw," he offered.

"He'll bring in another liar," Cogwell shouted. Fargo said nothing and in moments the footsteps sounded outside the door. Everyone's eyes were on the door as Caryn strode in. Her eyes went to Cogwell, icy fury in their hazel glare.

"Surprise," she slid at him. "Look who's alive."

Cogwell's jaw dropped open, the color drained from his face as he stared in shock at the slender figure before him. His lips worked but no sound came from them. "This is General Cogwell's daughter," Miles said.

"Disappointed, Daddy?" Caryn said to Cogwell, icy sarcasm coating each word. She turned to Elliman. "You must excuse my father. He thought I was dead. You see, he arranged for that to happen."

"Good God," Elliman whispered as he faced her.

"He sent her chained in a van, six troopers riding guard, into country filled with rampaging Pawnee," Miles said. "They'd all have been killed if Fargo hadn't happened by."

"Lies, more lies," Cogwell shouted but he was shaking now, his face ghostly.

Miles called out. "Please come in here, Lieutenant Roswall," he said, and the lieutenant stepped into the room. "Will you tell Secretary Elliman what I just told him is true?" Miles said.

"Absolutely true, sir," Roswall said.

"I'll have you up on charges, you bastard," Cogwell screamed at Roswall.

"You sent us all to die. It was a sure thing and it would've been written off as one more Indian attack," Roswall said. "All to get rid of your own daughter. Go to hell, sir."

"I saw General Davis's troop request lying in the files, same as Fargo did," Caryn said to Elliman and shot an icy glance at Cogwell, disdain wrapped in fury. She returned her gaze to Elliman. "Everything General Davis said about him is true, and more. I'm ashamed to be his daughter. He's a monster."

Elliman turned to Cogwell and saw the truth in a face twisted with rage. "Bitch, goddamn little bitch," Cogwell screamed at Caryn.

"I've heard enough," Elliman cut in. "I'm relieving you of command of this fort, pending a full and proper hearing by a full jury of senior officers."

Cogwell continued to glare at Caryn. Finally he turned from her, his hands clenching and unclenching. He brought his face under control, even managed a half smile, and moved closer to Elliman. "You do what you think best, Mr. Secretary," he said almost diffidently, and moving a step closer he suddenly exploded. His left arm snapped around Elliman's neck and his right hand pressed his army-issue Colt into Elliman's temple. "Anybody moves and I'll blow his damn head off," Cogwell hissed. "Stand back, all of you. Clear away." Fargo moved back to the wall, Miles with him, and Horgan and Roswall stepped to one side of the doorway as Cogwell started forward with his hostage.

Fear held Howard Elliman's face, perspiration coating his forehead, the small mustache quivering as Cogwell began dragging him from the office, through the outside doorway. "Anybody comes after me, he's dead," Cogwell shouted. "Anybody even moves, he's dead." It was no idle boast, Fargo knew. Cogwell had snapped, his world had collapsed around him. He knew a proper trial would prove his guilt. He had nothing left now but to flee and someday have his vengeance. He would want that. Vengeance was important to the twisted, the ruthless, the maniacs. But before vengeance, escape.

Fargo stayed against the wall, Horgan and Roswall beside him. He heard the horse gallop away from outside the building and waited until the sound died away before he moved. He ran outside, where the scene was still hectic with the wounded and others finding ways to restore their lives. Miles came up behind him and called to a knot of troopers. "General Cogwell just hightailed it out of here," he said.

"Had a gun to a man's head," one of the soldiers said.

"Which way'd they go?" Miles asked.

"Don't know. Just saw him leave the fort," the soldier said. Miles turned to Fargo and shrugged unhappily.

"Doesn't much matter. We can't risk following him," Miles said.

Fargo glanced around, alarm suddenly shooting through him. "Caryn. Where's Caryn?" he asked. Horgan and Roswall exchanged worried glances.

"Don't know. I was watching Cogwell," Horgan said.

"She was there. I wasn't watching her," Roswall said.

"She's gone after him, dammit," Fargo said.

"Fool girl. She'll get the secretary killed," Miles said.

"No she won't," Fargo said. "She's going to kill Cogwell." He spun on his heel, raced to the Ovaro, and vaulted into the saddle. "I've got to stop her," he said and sent the horse into a gallop. He swept the ground outside the fort. Most of it was chewed up with hundreds of prints, ruts, and gouges. He sorted through them as the horse galloped, using all that he knew, all his lore and trail wisdom, all his instincts, all the little things that had imprinted themselves in his mind. The line of hoofprints took shape, cutting through all the rest as a straight line cuts through circles and whorls. He swung onto the line and followed it. He knew he was on target when the prints grew clearer away from the fort.

He rode to his left then, at the edge of a line of black oak that still let him see the prints. The horse was being pushed, he saw, its stride beginning to shorten. He didn't bother to try and find Caryn's trail. She was somewhere ahead, keeping sight of Cogwell until she found the moment to move in on him. The trail turned onto a road bordered by bur oak and Fargo raced after the prints. Peering ahead, he saw a shape on the road and slowed when the shape became Howard Elliman. The man pushed to his feet, grimacing in pain. "Thank God, thank God," he gasped as he saw Fargo. "He threw me off, didn't stop, just threw me off."

"You were slowing him down. He didn't need a hostage anymore. He thinks he's gotten away," Fargo said.

"I guess he has," Elliman said.

"He hasn't," Fargo said, his thoughts flashing to Caryn. He snapped his reins and the Ovaro leaped forward.

"Wait. Don't leave me here," Elliman called.

"Be back," Fargo said and bent low in the saddle as the pinto raced forward. The road curved a few thousand yards ahead and Fargo slowed the horse, turning into the edge of the oaks and going forward carefully. He caught the sound of Cogwell's voice first, then Caryn's, and he spurred the horse forward, bursting out of the trees at the curve. Cogwell and Caryn were both on foot, Caryn holding the army Colt pointed at the general. She flicked a glance at Fargo as he burst onto the scene and swung from the Ovaro. Cogwell's pistol lay on the ground, a dozen yards away.

"Get away," she said as she brought her eyes back to Cogwell.

"Hold on," Fargo said calmly, stepping forward.

"No. He's going to get what he deserves," Caryn said and Fargo saw the fury in the tightness of her face. He took another step closer to Cogwell.

"Listen to me, Caryn. He'll get what he deserves," Fargo said.

"No he won't. He tried to kill me. I'm going to return the favor," Caryn hissed.

"Go ahead. I don't care, bitch," Cogwell said.

"I wouldn't do it if you didn't care," Caryn said. "But you care. That's why you tried to escape. You want to live. But I'm going to kill you for all the people you had killed, troopers, settlers, Indians."

Fargo sprang forward, a single, lightning-fast movement, and put himself in front of Cogwell, facing Caryn. "No," he said quietly. "Give me the gun."

She frowned at him. "Why are you doing this? You know what he's done. Why are you protecting him?"

"I'm not doing anything for him," Fargo said. "I don't want to save him. I want to save you."

She stared back. "From doing what ought to be done?" she threw at him.

"From your carrying this around the rest of your life," he said. "You will, you know. No matter how much you justify it to yourself, it won't wipe it out. You'll carry it forever. You don't need that. He'll have won again."

He saw the thoughts racing through her mind, her lips parted, rage and hate wrestling with a lifetime of compassion inside her. He had reached her, he knew, and he waited, letting her turn his words inside her again. "Put the gun down, Caryn. Let me take him back," he said softly. Her almost hazel eyes stared back and he saw them soften with the suddenness of a balloon losing air. She lowered her arm and let the pistol dangle from her fingertips. He was starting to reach out to her when the rush of sound exploded behind him. Cogwell slammed a shoulder into the middle of his back and Fargo felt the Colt yanked from his holster at the same instant.

He flung himself forward, slamming into Caryn in a tackle, and she went down with him as the shot whizzed over his head. Her gun fell from her hand and skittered away as Fargo rolled with her and Cogwell fired another shot. Coming against the trees, Fargo rolled into their protective foliage as Cogwell got off another shot that barely missed. "Stay down," he told Caryn, lifting his head a fraction. Cogwell was racing to his horse. He was in the saddle as Fargo ran from the trees, dropping as Cogwell sent another shot at him. He lay flat for a second and saw Cogwell racing off on his horse. Diving forward, he reached the Ovaro, vaulted onto the horse, and took after Cogwell.

He stayed low in the saddle, hanging back as Cogwell sent another shot at him. The general veered to his right, sending his horse across a stretch of open land that gave no chance for Fargo to close in without drawing a bullet. Edging the pinto forward as close as he dared, he stayed on Cogwell's tail. The man glanced back, his lips pulled back in a snarl, unwilling to fire the last two bullets in the Colt. Fargo pulled the lariat up and pushed the pinto a little closer. Cogwell glanced back and fired. Fargo ducked and yanked the pinto to his right. He took off after the other horse again, cursing into the wind. He could easily close in but Cogwell still had one shot left and one bullet was enough to end the chase. Cogwell knew the open land served to protect him; it made it impossible for Fargo to catch him in tree cover, and he veered his horse onto another stretch of wide prairie.

The army mount had stamina as did all army horses, Fargo realized, and the Ovaro had been subject to hard riding for the last night and day. He was afraid even the Ovaro's strength would begin to fade on a long chase across the prairie after a horse that had been stabled for the last three days. He made his decision, swearing at it but knowing he'd little choice. The Ovaro still had enough strength for a final burst of speed and Fargo spurred him on. As he stretched him out he could feel the pinto's power take hold. They closed in on Cogwell for a long minute and the man saw the pinto climbing up his rear. He raised the Colt, slowing his mount ever so slightly to steady his shot. As he did, Fargo swung his body almost out of the saddle in a trick-riding maneuver he had learned years ago and hadn't used since.

The wind pulled at him as he hung alongside the horse and he felt his weight pulling the Ovaro to the left. But he was below the level of the pinto's back and he heard the army mount's hoofbeats alongside him. He pulled himself upward, lifting himself for an instant. Cogwell was right alongside him. He fired but Fargo was already dropped back down against the side of the pinto. Using both feet as a springboard, he touched the ground. He remembered how to let the contact with the ground send him bouncing upward and into the saddle. Cogwell veered his horse away and Fargo saw the panic in his face. Pulling the pinto sideways with Cogwell, Fargo took his lariat again, twirled it upward, and sent it whirling through the air. Cogwell, trying to coax every last bit of speed from his horse, looked back just as the lariat descended on him.

He tried to duck away but the rope tightened around him. He flew from the saddle, across the horse's rump, and hit the ground. Fargo yanked the Ovaro to a halt at once and grimaced. He had felt the sharp pull on the rope and he swung from the saddle to stare down at Cogwell. The man's head lay twisted almost half around, his eyes staring lifelessly across the plains he had tried to turn into a blood red battleground. It was perhaps the most appropriate finish, Fargo reflected.

He took the lariat from around the man's neck, retrieved his Colt, and walked to where the army mount had come to a halt. Draping Cogwell facedown over his horse, Fargo climbed onto the Ovaro and began to retrace his steps across the plains. He'd gone halfway when Caryn rode toward him. She stared at the horse and its lifeless burden and wheeled her mount alongside Fargo. "Wanted to bring him back to stand trial. He hit the ground the wrong way, snapped his neck," Fargo said.

She nodded, riding silently beside him. Then she glanced back at the horse that followed. "Thanks," she said laconically.

"For this?" he asked.

"For not letting me do it," she said. He smiled and felt a satisfaction at words that meant more than they said. There were all kinds of victories.

They picked up Howard Elliman, took him back to the fort, and Caryn was beside Fargo as he said goodbye to Miles. "It's over but it's not the end of it," Miles said.

"No, not the end of it," Fargo agreed and Miles gave him a salute as he rode away with Caryn beside him.

"We avoided a massacre, a bloodbath. The fighting was contained. We bought some time," Fargo said.

"For what?" Caryn asked.

"For another day, another way for everyone. Maybe that's what life's all about, buying time to find a better day and a better way," Fargo said.

"And buying time to make love?" she said.

"That's the best kind to buy," he said. Her little smile told him they'd be proving that before the moon rose.

LOOKING FORWARD!
The following is the opening
section from the next novel in the exciting
Trailsman **series from Signet:**

THE TRAILSMAN #197
UTAH UPRISING

1861 . . . Southern Utah, where one man's lust
for power swept innocents up in a
whirlwind of bloodshed and slaughter . . .

The wilderness was full of surprises.

Skye Fargo had been traveling through some of the most rugged country west of the Mississippi for the better part of a week. After leaving Salt Lake City he had skirted the eastern edge of the Great Salt Lake Desert, an inferno unfit for man or beast. Once past the Sevier Plateau he had followed the Sevier River to the southeast, with majestic Mount Dutton rearing over ten thousand feet high on his left. Now he was in a spectacular region made up of rough, broad uplands slashed by deep canyons and isolated valleys, a region few white men ever visited.

So it was all the more puzzling to scale a ridge and see in the center of a low plain below a couple of buildings and a corral. Wisps of smoke curled lazily from a chimney and several dogs romped nearby.

Fargo's steely lake blue eyes narrowed. His brow knit. A big, broad-shouldered man, he sat the saddle as someone born to it, his muscular buckskin-clad frame hinting at the raw power in his limbs. Resting a hand on the Colt on his right hip, he reined down the ridge and across the dry plain. Overhead a hawk wheeled, inspecting him, then it screeched and soared off in search of prey.

The dogs stopped frolicking to watch his approach, their tails erect, their ears pricked. As he drew closer they moved to intercept his pinto stallion. Tongues lolling, teeth glistening in the bright sunlight, they planted themselves just past the corral and regarded him with open menace. As he came within earshot the dog in the middle growled. They were big brutes, sturdy mongrels with dark glittering eyes, the kind that could hold their own against a pack of wolves.

Fargo wrapped his palm around the Colt. He had dealt with vicious dogs before and knew that if they attacked they would go for the Ovaro's legs to bring the horse down. To show fear, to hesitate, invited a rush. Locking his gaze on the big leader, Fargo rode straight for them. He was well aware of the belief held by most mountain men that animals could be cowed by a human stare. It had been his experience that nine times out of ten the ruse worked, although exactly why was anybody's guess. Some claimed it was because the Almighty intended for man to be the masters of the beasts. Others felt it was due to the fact that a cold, hard stare was the mark of a fierce predator.

Whatever the reason, it worked again. The three mongrels slowly backed off, rumbling in their barrel chests, the leader snapping at empty air as if eager to grind his fangs on Fargo's bones. They retreated past the corral when suddenly the big one crouched and dug his claws into the ground, girding for a charge. Just then a woman cried out, "Fang, no!" From out of a ramshackle stable came a lithe Indian maiden who boldly marched up to the dogs and kicked one of them in the rump. All three backed off, but they were not happy about it.

Fargo's interest switched to his benefactor. She was young and lovely, her lush figure covered by a soft fawn-skin dress decorated with beads at the shoulders and neck. Raven hair, clipped short, was bound by a leather headband. Frank eyes regarded him with equal interest, and when he smiled in greeting she offered a shy grin in return. Cradled in her left arm was a bowl containing half a dozen eggs. "Thanks for lending a hand," he said. "I'd hate to have to shoot one of your dogs."

The woman bestowed a look on the trio that told Fargo she would not have minded one bit. "Fang, Slash, and Ripper are not mine," she answered in near-flawless English. Her voice was a throaty purr, and it sent a sensual tingle down the Trailsman's spine.

"Who do they belong to, then?"

From a porch attached to the second building a man answered. "They're mine, stranger. And if you get off that pinto of yours before I say you can, they'll eat you for dinner."

Fargo swiveled. The other building was as poorly built as the stable, but this one had a large sign over the porch that proclaimed to the whole world in crudely painted letters that it was CORNCOB BOB'S TRADING POST. Leaning on a spindly rail was a portly man in grimy clothes, who had an unlit corncob pipe jutting from the corner of his mouth. "Corncob Bob, I take it," Fargo said dryly.

"You reckon right, mister," declared the proprietor as he walked around the rail and stepped down. Out of the trading post ambled two more men, both as grubby as Corncob Bob. Human coyotes, if ever Fargo had seen any. The foremost was a tall drink of water who wore a Remington, butt forward on his left side. The second man, a small ratty specimen whose thin mustache resembled whiskers, sported a pair of Smith & Wesson revolvers in a wide belt adorned with silver studs. "Now suppose you tell me who you are and what you're doing here?"

Fargo turned the Ovaro so he was facing them. "Maybe you haven't heard, friend. But it's not considered polite in these parts to stick your nose into someone else's business."

Corncob Bob did not have a weapon that Fargo could see. Placing his pudgy hands on his ample stomach, he tilted his head to study Fargo a moment, then said amiably enough, "Don't get your hackles up, stranger. A man can't be too careful, is all. This territory is chock full of hardcases and badmen. For all I know, you could be out to rob me."

The two gunmen, Fargo noticed, had not left the

porch. They stood in the shadows, their thumbs hooked in their gunbelts, acting casual as could be but fooling no one. "All I'm interested in is some coffin varnish and a meal." He nodded at the stable. "And maybe some feed for my horse if you've got any to spare."

"I'm plumb out of oats but there's plenty of hay," Corncob Bob said. "Help yourself to a stall. The pitchfork is in the front corner." His flat gray eyes roved over the stallion, lingering on the saddle and the stock of the Henry that poked out from the long scabbard. "That's a fine rig you've got there. Been on the go a far piece to judge by all that dust."

"That I have," Fargo admitted. "And I never figured on finding a trading post way out here. Who do you get for customers? The Indians?"

The question must have reminded Corncob Bob of the maiden bearing the eggs. Turning toward her, he snapped, "What the hell are you doing just standing there, you lazy cuss? Didn't I give you a bunch of chores to do?" He raised a hand as if to slap her and she meekly bowed her head, making no effort to protect herself.

"I am sorry. But the dogs were about to attack this man."

"So you took it on yourself to interfere?" Corncob Bob grabbed her by the arm and shoved her toward the porch. "From now on just do as I tell you and let me worry about my dogs." He added a few oaths, then sighed and said to Fargo, "Damn squaw is more trouble than she's worth. It's all that education. She learned our tongue from a Bible thumper, and now she thinks we should treat her as an equal. Can you imagine that?"

Skye Fargo did not respond. Inside of him an icy knot had formed. He saw the two gunmen leer at the woman as she scurried inside. The ratlike man even had the gall to take a swipe at her backside, but she was too quick for him.

"As for the meal you're wanting," Corncob Bob had gone on, "I can have Sue whip up some eggs and venison. And to wash it down I'll treat you to some of the best sipping whiskey ever made. How would that be?"

"Just fine." Fargo reined the pinto to the left and entered the gloomy interior of the stable. It only held six stalls, four of which were filled. At the rear were about twenty chickens, clucking and pecking the ground or nestled snugly in cubbyholes set up for them to lay their eggs. A rooster sat on a bench, preening. A few yards from the bench was a small pen containing five noisy pigs. The place reeked of odors that would gag a member of polite society.

After stripping his saddle off, Fargo located the pitchfork and thrust it into a sizeable pile of hay. Soon he had heaped enough in front of the stallion. With his rifle tucked under an arm, he strolled to the trading post. The three dogs were by the corral, and not once did they take their eyes off him. No one was outside. Pausing at the steps, he scanned the stark mesas to the southeast and the Paunsagunt Plateau to the southwest. There was not another sign of human habitation anywhere.

The inside of the post was almost as dim as the stable. On the right a counter ran the length of the wall, on the left were two tables. The trade goods, such as they were, had been thrown into a single corner, blankets and pots and trinkets all jumbled together. Fargo took a seat, placing his chair so his back was to the wall and he could command a view of the entire room. He set his rifle on the table within easy reach.

Corncob Bob was behind the counter. The two gunmen were at the far end, drinking. Of the woman there was no sign, although faint sounds issued from a doorway at the rear. Fargo pushed the brim of his hat back and ran a hand over his chin. He wouldn't mind a bath, but from the looks of the owner, Corncob Bob had never used a tub in his life and wasn't likely to have one on the premises.

Through the doorway hustled the maiden, her chin tucked to her chest, her hands folded at her waist. She had the air of a frightened doe. Avoiding the two gunmen, she came to Fargo's table. "Pardon me. But how would you like your eggs and steak?" she timidly asked, while out of the corner of her eyes she peeked at the counter where Corncob Bob was treating himself to a drink right from the bottle.

"You're Sue?" Fargo said. He had assumed the trader referred to a white woman, possibly his wife.

"It is the name he has given me," the maiden said, jabbing a slender figure at the slovenly figure. "He finds it too hard to say my real one."

"What is it?"

Before the woman could reply, Corncob Bob smacked the whiskey bottle onto the counter and bellowed, "What's all the jabbering, girl? Just find out what he wants and fix it. And don't dally, if you know what's good for you."

Terror flared in the maiden's eyes, genuine, unbridled fear so potent she blanched and nervously wrung her fingers. Fargo was going to ask why she was so scared but he did not want the trader to grow any madder at her than he already was. Besides, for all Fargo knew, Sue *was* the man's wife. Maybe not in a strictly legal sense, with a swapping of vows and a ring. But many a frontiersman had taken up with an Indian woman, sometimes out of love, more often out of lust. It was a sad fact that quite a few tribes allowed their maidens to be bartered for, or outright bought. "Scrambled eggs and a rare steak will do," he told her.

Nodding, she scampered off. But as she passed the two gunmen, the rat-faced man's hand flicked out faster than the darting tongue of a snake and closed on her wrist, jerking her up short.

"What's your rush, darlin'? Why don't you let Rufus and me treat you to some firewater?"

"I have a meal to cook," Sue said and tried to pull her arm loose, but the gunman would not let go.

"It can wait."

"Please, Mr. Lafferty. You're hurting me." The woman took a step back and wrenched mightily but only succeeded in causing herself more pain. She glanced at Corncob Bob in mute appeal. All he did was tip the bottle and gulp great mouthfuls, half the whiskey spilling over his fleshy jowls and trickling down his thick neck.

"What's wrong with a little pain, sweetheart?" Lafferty said with relish. "It's more fun that way." Shifting, he pulled her against him and held her close. She thrashed and wriggled, becoming more and more desperate, to no avail.

Corncob Bob lowered the bottle and belched. "Lafferty, you know the rules. You can't manhandle the squaw like that. Fork over five dollars first or go out to the stable and fondle that ornery mare of yours."

Rufus had reached up to run his fingers through the maiden's hair. "It's been a coon's age since I had me a female. How about both of us at once, Bob? How much would that come to?"

"Can't you add? Ten dollars."

"We should get a discount," Rufus said. "Be a nice guy and shave some off since we're good pards and all. I've only got two dollars on me, plus some change. I suppose I could throw in my watch, even though it's busted."

Corncob Bob moved down the counter. "This ain't no charity, you peckerwood. What in the world would I do with a broken watch? I don't ever care what time it is." Extending his left palm, he wagged it under their noses. "Ten dollars, you two, and that's final. Don't raise a fuss, either, or Pike will hear of it."

The men were so intent on haggling that none of them paid any attention to Fargo. Rising with the Henry in his left hand, he wound past the tables and around a stack of blankets and other merchandise, coming up on the gunmen from the rear. The maiden was still striving to free herself from Lafferty's grasp and happened to see him. Her eyes widened when she saw his expression and she shook her head as if to warn him off. But Fargo did not heed. Planting himself squarely, he declared, "Mind if I have a say?"

Lafferty and Rufus both turned, neither anticipating trouble. The former frowned, then started to open his mouth. It was then that Fargo drove the Henry's stock into Lafferty's side with such force that Lafferty was jolted backward, crashing into the counter and half sprawling across it. Rufus, belatedly, snorted like an irate bull buffalo and clawed for his Remington, but he was pathetically slow, molasses in motion. Fargo swept the Henry's barrel up and around, clipping Rufus across the temple. The tall gunman crumpled like a sheet of paper and lay on his side, a scarlet rivulet seeping from a nasty gash.

Corncob Bob was agape in astonishment. His thick lips worked like those of a carp out of water, and it was a full ten seconds before he collected his wits and blurted, "What do you think you're doing, mister? I don't allow no rough stuff in my place."

Fargo leveled the Henry, the muzzle inches from the trader's huge belly. "You didn't object to these two polecats roughing up the girl."

"Why should I? She's a mangy squaw." Corncob Bob's forehead glistened with beads of sweat. "What are you, anyway? Some kind of Injun lover, or something?" His forefinger speared at the woman. "I'll have you know she's mine to do with as I darn well please. Just a couple of weeks ago I gave her pa a heap of trinkets so she could come and live with me for a year."

Fargo's dislike of the man increased by leaps and bounds. The poor maiden was quaking like an aspen leaf in a gale, and he read in her gaze the gratitude she did not utter aloud. "What I am is starved."

Corncob Bob glanced at the Henry. His Adam's apple bobbed and he mustered a wan smile. "Sure, mister, sure. I don't want no trouble. I'll have the boys wait until after you're done." To the girl he hissed, "Get cracking, instead of standing there like a bump on a log. Be sure and fix everything proper, too, or there will be hell to pay."

The maiden nodded and went to leave.

"Hold on," Fargo said. "You never told me your real name."

"Winnemucca."

She was gone in a flash, with a swirl of her hair and a hint of a friendly smile, as graceful as an antelope, as beautiful as a spring day. Fargo felt a familiar hunger that had nothing to do with food, and a stirring in his loins.

"Stupid Injun names," Corncob Bob said. "Who can pronounce those tongue twisters? I call her Sue, after a cow my pa had on our farm back in Ohio when I was a boy. Come to think of it, Injuns are about as dumb as cows, ain't they?"

Fargo nearly lost his self-control. He came so close to slamming the Henry into the trader's vile mouth that he had to back away. Rufus was out cold, but Lafferty had shaken off the effects of the blow to his rib cage and was uncurling, hatred contorting his rodent features. The small gunman's hands hovered over the Smith & Wesson.

"Nobody does that to me and gets away with it. Put

down that rifle, hombre, and let's see how tough you really are."

Rather than indulge the killer, Fargo pointed the Henry at Lafferty's chest. "You've got it backwards. Shuck the gunbelt and let it drop. After I leave you can pick it up again. But if you so much as touch it before then—" Fargo thumbed back the hammer to emphasize his point.

Lafferty was livid, a living powder keg primed to explode. His fingers clenched and unclenched and he grit his teeth in a feral snarl. "I don't take my guns off for anyone."

"Suit yourself," Fargo said and fired into the front of the counter a hand's width to the gunman's left. Corncob Bob squealed and jumped, but Lafferty did not so much as bat an eye. "The next one will go right through you." Again Fargo curled back the hammer, and when it clicked, the hardcase promptly shed his hardware, letting them *thunk* onto the floor.

"You'll pay, you son of a bitch. Mark my words."

Fargo did not doubt for a moment he had made a bitter enemy and that Lafferty would try to make worm food of him at the earliest opportunity. A smart man would shoot the gunman dead on the spot. Or so Fargo sought to convince himself. But he had never gunned down an unarmed person in his life, and he was not about to start. Having scruples had its drawbacks, he reflected. "Any time you feel man enough."

Lafferty glared as Fargo returned to his chair. If looks could kill, the gunman would have shriveled Fargo like a withered plant.

Rufus stirred to life and sluggishly sat up. "What in tarnation happened?" he mumbled, blankly blinking. Then he stiffened and gingerly touched the gash. "Now I remember." Heaving to his feet, he swung toward the tables. "You hit me, you varmint."

Fargo already had the Henry pointed in the right direction. Elevating it a hair, he casually asked, "Ever seen what a .44-caliber slug can do to a man's insides?"

Rufus had not seemed to realize the rifle was trained on him until that moment. Taking a step backward, he hiked up both arms and bleated, "Now hold on there, stranger. Maybe I was a mite hasty. Let's forget the whole thing, shall we?"

The plea was as counterfeit as fool's gold. The tall hardcase was not the sort to forgive and forget, and they both knew it. Fargo had been in similar situations too many times to be fooled. The two buzzards would bide their time and bushwhack him when it suited them. "Do like your friend did and shed the six-shooter."

It was remarkable how swiftly a man could unbuckle a belt when properly motivated. Rufus slowly lowered it, careful not to scrape the Remington. As he straightened, he remarked, "I never did catch your handle, mister."

"I never mentioned it." Fargo laid the rifle down and pretended to ignore the pair as they huddled and whispered, no doubt making plans to execute their revenge. Both cast repeated smoldering glances his way. Corncob Bob, chewing on the stem of his pipe, came over bearing the whiskey bottle and set it on the edge of the table.

"Here you go, friend. Wait until you taste this tornado juice. It goes down as smooth as can be."

The trader's spittle was dribbling over the label. Fargo did not even bother to pick it up. "Fetch a new bottle."

"Huh? What's wrong with this one?"

"Nothing a ton of lye soap couldn't cure." Fargo leaned back and waited while the heavyset proprietor complied. His thoughts drifted to Camp Douglas, an army post situated on a bench overlooking Salt Lake City. The federal government had established it to protect the Overland mail and telegraph and keep tabs on hostiles, or so the politicians claimed. But they weren't fooling a soul. The real reason the post had been set up was so the government could keep a tight rein on the Mormons.

A week ago Fargo had stopped there on his trek east and had encountered an old acquaintance, Colonel Tom O'Neil. That evening as they sat reminiscing about their Arizona days O'Neil had abruptly changed the subject. "Ever hear of the Chemehuevi tribe?"

Fargo had. Whites called them the Southern Paiutes, or Digger Indians, a derogatory nickname. It stemmed from the practice of the Chemehuevi men carrying pointed sticks used to pry wild vegetables and roots from the soil. Foragers, they roamed the land in small bands, barely eking out a living. They were a poor tribe—the poorest of the poor. Fargo had never had any personal dealings with the Chemehuevi, although he had run into their kin, the Northern Paiutes, on occasion. "What about them?"

O'Neil had fidgeted, acting uncomfortable about bringing up the subject. "I know about the time you spent among the Sioux when you were young. It explains why you've always been friendly to the Indians, why you're not one of those who believes that the only good redskin is a dead redskin." Pausing, he had toyed with a button on his uniform. "I really have no business imposing on you, but word has leaked back to me that the Chemehuevi are having a hard time of it."

When Fargo offered no comment, the officer continued. "I'd look into the rumors myself, but I have my hands full with the Mormons. There is talk of another rebellion, in case you haven't heard. And all because our government won't let them practice polygamy any longer." Catching himself, O'Neil said, "But back to the Chemehuevis. Their problem doesn't really fall under military jurisdiction. Nor will the civil authorities look into it unless they receive complaints and—"

"What exactly is the problem?" Fargo had interrupted.

O'Neil leaned forward. "Vague reports have filtered to me through some of my scouts. Reports of Chemehuevis being beaten and whipped, and of a chief who was hung. I know it's none of your affair, but I was hoping you could look into the situation and get word to me if it's as bad as it seems."

So here Fargo was, seated in a trading post in the heart of Chemehuevi territory, a trading post that had no business being there. Not if Corncob Bob counted on making a living at it. No trappers roamed the nearby mountains, no settlers or ranchers lived in the vicinity. In short, there was no one with whom Bob could trade other than the poverty-stricken Chemehuevis. Fargo's reverie ended as the trader deposited a new bottle at his elbow. "Much obliged."

The whiskey was everything the man had claimed. It burned a path clear down to Fargo's stomach, warming him through and through. Shortly thereafter the food arrived. Winnemucca brought it on a large tray, deftly balanced on her head. The eggs and steak had been done to perfection, and Fargo savored his first bite of each.

"It is all right?" Winnemucca asked hopefully, anxious to please. Up close he could not avoid noticing how her bosom swelled against her dress, and the shapely outline of her hips and thighs. It was enough to set his loins to twitching again.

"Better than that. This is downright delicious." Fargo motioned at the chair across from his. "Have a seat. I'd like some company."

Winnemucca stole a glance at the counter. Corncob Bob had overheard and gave a vigorous shake of his moon head. "I cannot, sir, as much as I would like to. I may only talk to customers when they have paid for the privilege. It is one of Mr. Newton's many rules."

"Rules be hanged." Fargo nudged the chair with the tip of a boot. "Sit a spell. I'm after some information and you might be able to help." He took another swallow. "Have you by any chance heard of a Chemehuevi chief being hung by white men?" That was all O'Neil had been able to tell him. No name, no location, no other details.

A hush descended. Lafferty and Rufus stopped whispering and glanced around so sharply they were in danger of throwing their necks out. Corncob Bob Newton froze in the act of reaching for a glass. Winnemucca recoiled as if she had been slapped and lost all the color in her sun-bronzed cheeks. Much too quickly she said, "No, I have not. Now if you will excuse me."

Fargo was out of his chair before she had gone two steps. Lightly gripping her arm, he said, "Hold on. I need to get at the truth. I won't let any harm come to you, if that's what you're afraid of."

Winnemucca placed a warm hand on his. "Please. Whoever you are. You have been kind to me, so I will give you advice you must take. Finish your meal and go before you get into a lot of trouble."

"Too late for that, squaw," said Corncob Bob.

Skye Fargo shifted to tell the trader to mind his own business. The words died on the tip of his tongue at the sight of a double-barreled shotgun fixed on his midsection. At that range the scattergun would blow him in half.

⦿ SIGNET

MORE EXCITING ACTION
FROM THE TRAILSMAN SERIES

☐ **THE TRAILSMAN #161: ROGUE RIVER FEUD by Jon Sharpe.** When Skye Fargo arrived in Oregon's Rogue River Valley, he couldn't understand why every gun was against him until he came face to face with his own devilish double—the deadly Dunn. Fargo was up against a man who was more than his match when it came to murder. (182189—$3.99)

☐ **THE TRAILSMAN #162: REVENGE AT LOST CREEK by Jon Sharpe.** Skye Fargo had to watch his back with a pack of men who would do anything and kill anyone for wealth . . . he had to watch his step with women ready, eager and willing to get on his good side by getting in his arms . . . and he had to watch a nightmare plan of revenge coming true no matter how fast he moved and how straight he shot. (182197—$3.99)

☐ **THE TRAILSMAN #163: YUKON MASSACRE by Jon Sharpe.** Skye Fargo was in the most god-forsaken wilderness in North America—Russian Alaska, where the only thing more savage than nature was man. Fargo had to lead a cutthroat crew on a hunt for a missing beauty named Natasha and the murderous men who held her captive. Now it was up to Fargo to find his way through the blizzard of lies to a secret that chilled him to the bone. (182200—$3.99)

☐ **THE TRAILSMAN #164: NEZ PERCE NIGHTMARE by Jon Sharpe.** Skye Fargo just can't say no when duty and desire call. That's why he finds himself dodging bullets from bushwhackers as he hunts a mysterious foe bent on building a Rocky Mountain empire with white corpses and redskin blood. (182219—$3.99)

*Prices slightly higher in Canada

Buy them at your local bookstore or use this convenient coupon for ordering.

PENGUIN USA
P.O. Box 999 — Dept. #17109
Bergenfield, New Jersey 07621

Please send me the books I have checked above.
I am enclosing $_____ (please add $2.00 to cover postage and handling). Send check or money order (no cash or C.O.D.'s) or charge by Mastercard or VISA (with a $15.00 minimum). Prices and numbers are subject to change without notice.

Card #_____ Exp. Date _____
Signature_____
Name_____
Address_____
City _____ State _____ Zip Code _____

For faster service when ordering by credit card call **1-800-253-6476**

Allow a minimum of 4-6 weeks for delivery. This offer is subject to change without notice.

Ⓞ SIGNET

LEGENDS OF THE WEST

☐ **SCARLET PLUME by Frederick Manfred.** Amid the bloody 1862 Sioux uprising, a passion that crosses all boundaries is ignited. Judith Raveling is a white woman captured by the Sioux Indians. Scarlet Plume, nephew of the chief who has taken Judith for a wife, is determined to save her. But surrounded by unrelenting brutal fighting and vile atrocities, can they find a haven for a love neither Indian nor white woman would sanction?
(184238—$4.50)

☐ **WHITE APACHE by Frank Burleson.** Once his name was Nathanial Barrington, one of the finest officers in the United States Army. Now his visions guide him and his new tribe on daring raids against his former countrymen. Amid the smoke of battle and in desire's fiercest blaze, he must choose between the two proud peoples who fight for his loyalty and the two impassioned women who vie for his soul. (187296—$5.99)

☐ **WHISPERS OF THE RIVER by Tom Hron.** Passion and courage, greed and daring—a stirring saga of the Alaskan gold rush. With this rush of brawling, lusting, striving humanity, walked Eli Bonnet, a legendary lawman who dealt out justice with his gun ... and Hannah Twigg, a woman who dared death for love and everything for freedom. (187806—$5.99)

*Prices slightly higher in Canada   **WA39X**

Buy them at your local bookstore or use this convenient coupon for ordering.

PENGUIN USA
P.O. Box 999 — Dept. #17109
Bergenfield, New Jersey 07621

Please send me the books I have checked above.
I am enclosing $_____ (please add $2.00 to cover postage and handling). Send check or money order (no cash or C.O.D.'s) or charge by Mastercard or VISA (with a $15.00 minimum). Prices and numbers are subject to change without notice.

Card #_____ Exp. Date _____
Signature_____
Name_____
Address_____
City _____ State _____ Zip Code _____

For faster service when ordering by credit card call **1-800-253-6476**

Allow a minimum of 4-6 weeks for delivery. This offer is subject to change without notice.

SIGNET (0451)

BLAZING NEW TRAILS WITH THE ACTION-PACKED TRAILSMAN SERIES BY JON SHARPE

☐ THE TRAILSMAN #125: BLOOD PRAIRIE (172388—$3.50)
☐ THE TRAILSMAN #137: MOON LAKE MASSACRE (175948—$3.50)
☐ THE TRAILSMAN #141: TOMAHAWK JUSTICE (177525—$3.50)
☐ THE TRAILSMAN #142: GOLDEN BULLETS (177533—$3.50)
☐ THE TRAILSMAN #143: DEATHBLOW TRAIL (177541—$3.50)
☐ THE TRAILSMAN #144: ABILENE AMBUSH (177568—$3.50)
☐ THE TRAILSMAN #151: CROW HEART'S REVENGE (178874—$3.50)
☐ THE TRAILSMAN #152: PRAIRIE FIRE (178882—$3.99)
☐ THE TRAILSMAN #155: OKLAHOMA ORDEAL (178912—#3.99)
☐ THE TRAILSMAN #156: SAWDUST TRAIL (181603—#3.99)
☐ THE TRAILSMAN #157: GHOST RANCH MASSACRE (181611—$3.99)
☐ THE TRAILSMAN #158: TEXAS TERROR (182154—$3.99)
☐ THE TRAILSMAN #159: NORTH COUNTRY GUNS (182162—#3.99)
☐ THE TRAILSMAN #160: TORNADO TRAIL (182170—$3.99)

Prices slightly higher in Canada **W54X**

Buy them at your local bookstore or use this convenient coupon for ordering.

PENGUIN USA
P.O. Box 999 — Dept. #17109
Bergenfield, New Jersey 07621

Please send me the books I have checked above.
I am enclosing $_____ (please add $2.00 to cover postage and handling). Send check or money order (no cash or C.O.D.'s) or charge by Mastercard or VISA (with a $15.00 minimum). Prices and numbers are subject to change without notice.

Card #_____ Exp. Date _____
Signature_____
Name_____
Address_____
City _____ State _____ Zip Code _____

For faster service when ordering by credit card call **1-800-253-6476**

Allow a minimum of 4-6 weeks for delivery. This offer is subject to change without notice.

Ⓞ SIGNET

THE APACHE WARS TRILOGY BY FRANK BURLESON

☐ **DESERT HAWKS.** This enthralling first novel in *The Apache Wars* trilogy captures the drama and real history of a struggle in which no side wanted to surrender ... in a series alive with all the excitement and adventure of brave men and women—white and Native American—who decided the future of America.   (180895—$4.50)

☐ **WAR EAGLES.** First Lieutenant Nathanial Barrington was about to undergo his first test as a professional soldier following orders he distrusted in an undeclared war—as well as his test as a man when he met the Apache woman warrior Jocita in a night lit by passion that would yield to a day of dark decision.   (180909—$4.50)

☐ **SAVAGE FRONTIER.** First Lieutenant Nathanial Barrington was already a battle-scarred veteran of the Apache Wars, but nothing in his fighting life as a soldier prepared him for the violence sweeping over the southwest in the greatest test the U.S. Army ever faced, and the hardest choice Barrington ever had to make.   (180917—$4.99)

☐ **WHITE APACHE** Once his name was Nathanial Barrington, one of the finest officers in the United States Army. Now his visions guide him and his new tribe on daring raids against his former countrymen. Amid the smoke of battle and in desire's fiercest blaze, he must choose between the two proud peoples who fight for his loyalty and the two impassioned women who vie for his soul.   (187296—$5.99)

*Prices slightly higher in Canada

Buy them at your local bookstore or use this convenient coupon for ordering.

PENGUIN USA
P.O. Box 999 — Dept. #17109
Bergenfield, New Jersey 07621

Please send me the books I have checked above.
I am enclosing $_____ (please add $2.00 to cover postage and handling). Send check or money order (no cash or C.O.D.'s) or charge by Mastercard or VISA (with a $15.00 minimum). Prices and numbers are subject to change without notice.

Card #_____ Exp. Date _____
Signature_____
Name_____
Address_____
City _____ State _____ Zip Code _____

For faster service when ordering by credit card call **1-800-253-6476**

Allow a minimum of 4-6 weeks for delivery. This offer is subject to change without notice.

Ⓒ SIGNET CLASSIC   (0451)

LIFE ON THE FRONTIER

☐ **THE CALL OF THE WILD and Selected Stories by Jack London.** Foreword by Franklin Walker. The American author's vivid picture of the wild life of a dog and a man in the Alaskan gold fields.
(523903—$3.95)

☐ **THE DEERSLAYER by James Fenimore Cooper.** The classic frontier saga of an idealistic youth, raised among the Indians, who emerges to face life with a nobility as pure and proud as the wilderness whose fierce beauty and freedom have claimed his heart.
(524845—$5.95)

☐ **THE OX-BOW INCIDENT by Walter Van Tilburg Clark.** A relentlessly honest novel of violence and quick justice in the Old West. Afterword by Walter Prescott Webb.
(525256—$5.95)

Prices slightly higher in Canada.   **W10X**

Buy them at your local bookstore or use this convenient coupon for ordering.

PENGUIN USA
P.O. Box 999 — Dept. #17109
Bergenfield, New Jersey 07621

Please send me the books I have checked above.
I am enclosing $_____ (please add $2.00 to cover postage and handling). Send check or money order (no cash or C.O.D.'s) or charge by Mastercard or VISA (with a $15.00 minimum). Prices and numbers are subject to change without notice.

Card #_____ Exp. Date _____
Signature_____
Name_____
Address_____
City _____ State _____ Zip Code _____

For faster service when ordering by credit card call **1-800-253-6476**

Allow a minimum of 4-6 weeks for delivery. This offer is subject to change without notice.